"IT HAD A HEAD, WITH A RED SLASH ON EACH SIDE OF ITS CHEEKS. AND EYES. LOOKING AT US. THE MOUTH OPENED, AND ALGAE FELL FROM THE BEAK—OR JAWS—THAT HUNG OPEN, HISSING. IT BEGAN TO PADDLE WITH TWO HUGE FRONT PAWS, WITH NAILS LIKE TALONS, PUSHING AT THE SCUM. THE PAWS CAME UP ONE AT A TIME, ONTO THE LEDGE BY OUR FEET. THEN THE THING LUNGED UP, DRIPPING SLIME. . ."

This was the first of the creatures. It was not the last by far.

Or the worst.

Don't even try to guess what *that* was. . . .

DEATH TOUR

"Fascinating horror . . . a shocker . . . you can't put it down until you discover the horrible secrets that you'll never forget!"
—*Chattanooga News-Free Press*

"GORY ACTION . . . SOMETHING SPECIAL!"
—*Kirkus Reviews*

More Suspense from SIGNET

* Price slightly higher in Canada
† Not available in Canada

To order these titles,
please use coupon on the
last page of this book.

DEATH TOUR

TOUR

by
David
J.
Michael

A SIGNET BOOK
NEW AMERICAN LIBRARY
TIMES MIRROR

PUBLISHED BY
THE NEW AMERICAN LIBRARY
OF CANADA LIMITED

For the folks on the L Taraval

Death
Tour

One

Imagination.

We needed something fresh—something even wilder than the news stories we'd been running. We'd formed a little campus production group called Five-Star, and we were a hit, but we'd worked ourselves into a corner. The more successful our regular feature *Touring* became, the more desperate we became for material.

Three years of journalistic triumph. We'd started out with "The Pigeon Lady," our story of the little old woman who religiously spread fifty pounds of bird seed and bread crumbs on various street corners every day, to preserve one of America's vanishing species, the pigeon;

Followed by our two-edition exposé on the heavy witchcraft traffic springing up out in the suburbs;

Followed by "Good Night, Irene," an evening tour with a downtown hooker;

The Church Bingo Scandals;

Not to mention "What's in Your Soup?"—the consumer tour of our famous cannery. Followed by "What's in Your Bread?"—the local bakery;

1

Plus Krevitch's series of candid shots, "Outtakes," the best of which was the mayor, caught trapped in a pay toilet.

But it got to be a problem. The Success Syndrome. Where to go from here? You couldn't enter a lecture room anymore without six people asking what the next *Touring* was going to expose—and we didn't have the slightest. We'd already collected a handful of Disciplinary Warnings from the Dean's Office over even our milder offerings, and now some of the suggestions pouring into the Journalism Building from overzealous fans were nothing short of obscene. A couple times we'd thought of quitting while we were ahead—there being no place to go but insane—but each time, the editor of the *Varsity Press* himself would beg us to stay on. He swore it was the only thing anyone on campus bothered to read anymore. Everyone was bored, it seemed, with sorority teas and the Sweetheart of Sigma Chi and the Blood Drive and Professor Krutch receiving the Westinghouse Engineer of the Year Award.

Which we'd anticipated when we'd first started out, of course. That's why we'd called it *Touring* meaning far out, trippy.

But not Kink City.

Dear Five-Star:
How about covering the homosexual hustlers on Four Ave.? Should be a good story.
Sincerely,
Interested

"No," Krevitch squeaked in his tiny, terrible voice. He squirmed and looked around. A few of the more unkind elements on campus had dubbed him Rodent, but I always liked Krevitch. "Not after 'Good Night, Irene.' We'll get suspended."

"Try another one," I said.

Cherry ripped open the envelope and read loudly to the entire building, like someone at the Academy Awards:

> Dear Five-Star:
> Interview the little grocer just off-campus, Harkins Ave., & Second. Gangland executions.
> A Friend

Cherry shuddered. "That'll be our last story," she said. Every pencil and clipboard on the staff table shuddered, too. Cherry filled up three-quarters of one side of the long table. When she rocked, the room rocked with her. She turned the letter over with a slam.

And we tried another one.

> Dear Five-Star:
> How about covering an abortion, from begining to end?
> Avid Reader

"Next," I said.

> Dear Five-Star:
> Hermaphrodites. Could you interview one?
> Curious

"What's a—what's—a herma—what?" Hunk asked. He studied the word very carefully and silently, as if it were a rare beetle perched on the paper. The skin on his protruding forehead wrinkled. Hunk wasn't retarded, as some said. But he was slow.

"I think," I said, flipping my fingers through the pile, "that it's time to strike out on a new path."

"And I think," Mary, last of the Five, said, "that I've got to strike out on an old path. Home." She stood up tall, with big cool eyes. "Want to walk me?"

"Sure," I answered, and stood up too. Mary was pale, and bone blonde. She always looked a little withdrawn, and she always looked a little sad.

"Wait a goddamn minute!" Cherry burst out. "What do we do for a *story?*" When no one answered, she jammed a pencil into her red afro and said, "Okay! Then we go with The Molester!"

"No more sickies," I said.

"You got a better idea?" She leaned forward on her mammoth elbows. The table groaned. She just sat there, leering and obese, until she looked a little like some kind of Molester herself—someone you might run into outside a park lavatory.

I had to admit I didn't have.

"Either that or close shop," she finished.

It sounded so final.

Krevitch twitched and jerked, and Hunk sank deeper into his habitual coma. Cherry herself looked as though she'd collapse right through that table. Mary gazed at me, a little vacantly and sadly, and I—I liked our hard-earned fame. It was a kind of campus participation. Fitting in, making it, a link with the rest of the student body, when ordinarily we'd never have had any link at all. I hated to see it all phase out.

"We'll think of something," I said quickly, trying to inspire everyone to our old heights. "Something interesting, only—you know—not sick."

"No such animal,". Cherry answered. "Sex or violence. That's all there is."

"Or comedy," Krevitch added.

Hunk burped.

"I'll figure out something," I said, gathering my books and notes. "Don't worry."

Cherry ignored me, always the diehard. She started in on those letters again. "Dear Five-Star," she read, even louder:

> Statistics show seventy-five percent of homicides are committed within families. Why not an in-depth feature—

"Come on," I said to Mary.

"Hahahaha!" Cherry boomed, like a truckdriver. She tried to pick it up again.

"Why not an in-depth feature on that *laugh?*" I asked. That just made her roar even more, and everyone in the office, too. In fact, the entire journalism staff was looking now. They all thought we were insane, of course. But they were all curious, too—just as curious as everyone else on that campus, wondering exactly what the next Five-Star feature would be. . . .

Two

There were a few shops off-campus, just before the avenues.

"Want a frozen yogurt?" I asked. Our favorite health food.

She looked at the line of two or three people. "I can't," she said. "I've got to get home."

"Boysenberry," I tried.

"I can't stop."

"It'll just take a second."

"I've got to get home."

So we walked on. I don't think she ever realized how many times a day she used that expression. She always *had to get home*. She went to school, to get home. She went out to the store, to get home. If she was doing staff work on the newspaper, or grabbing a hamburger—even if we were in the sack—she always had to speed it up, to get home. It bothered me as we were walking, but I don't think she noticed. Mary was always a little preoccupied—with home, of course. She had a father who lived in the house all alone, who had somehow convinced her that she should spend the rest of her natural life caring for him, obeying him, and serving him. It was almost to the point of sickness. No. It was to the point of sickness.

Which is why I said, "Maybe I do have an idea for *Touring!*"

"What?" She wasn't really listening, just walking dreamily, enjoying the good spring outside air while she could.

"We'll call it 'The Mad Dad.' "

She didn't get it. "About who?"

"The Fanatical Father—who's completely possessive of his daughter. She's twenty, but she can't date, she can't stay out late, she can't even have telephone calls coming in. He monitors her life."

Amazing, but she still didn't get it. She just looked at me quizzically, toying with a dandelion she'd picked up along the way. There was something in Mary that wouldn't let her break out—something beaten or browbeaten right into her.

"He lives alone in this big house," I continued—and I think she suddenly got it. I didn't look at her face; I just continued. "He's driven away everyone—his wife, friends, even the neighbors. He lives behind this ugly six-foot-high solid-board fence."

"All right, stop it," she said.

"He's a compulsive worker—fourteen, sixteen hours a day, seven days a week. He's the plant superintendent, so there's a perfect excuse for him to be there at all times, even on his days off. He wants complete control—over everything—so much that he's alienated half the workers and has actually reduced his staff to a skeleton crew. And even those few have a hard time just doing their jobs now, because he demands that everything be done His Way."

She was crying a little. Mary always did cry very easily. "You don't know my father," she said. "You don't know what he's been through. He's lonely. He's never been the same since my mother left."

I didn't push it. I did know her father. I'd known him since I'd known Mary, three years, since first semester freshman year. Mr. Malgren loathed me. He wouldn't even let me into the house. He wouldn't let me phone her. He'd destroy the letters and cards I wrote her. But Mary always insisted that it wasn't me, that he was that way with everyone—as if that made it more tolerable.

She breathed in very deeply, so deeply that I thought she was sighing. But she was just changing the subject.

"God," she said, "isn't it beautiful out here?"

It was. It was daylight saving time now, and still sunny and warm at six P.M. All the lawns on the avenues were green and thick with flower borders and shrubs. Water sprinklers were going, and there was the sweet smell of pine and honeysuckle. A few far-off kids' voices cut through the quiet. It was so peaceful that you could hear your own footsteps on the sidewalk.

I hated to see her street come up.

"Let's take off somewhere tonight," I said.

She just looked at me. She wanted to, you could see it. She had the world's clearest, bluest eyes.

Ice-blue. Moonstone blue. And hair as white as bone.

"I can't," she said.

"I know. You've got to stay home."

"I really do." She touched my hand with her long fingers.

"Your father needs you," I added.

"He really does."

"You have to cook his dinner. Then do the laundry. Then go out and get some shopping done. And clean the house. And—"

"He does some of those things himself," she said. "But tonight he really does need some help."

"He's entertaining the mayor for dinner," I guessed. "They're going to discuss the new atomic sewer plant."

"You know the mayor's still locked in the pay toilet," she answered—one of her rare flashes of humor. I had to laugh out loud. I almost squeezed her. A ray of hope. But she snapped right back to her old preoccupation.

"He hurt himself at work," she said.

"He fell into the settling tank," I tried. Mary's father worked at the town's waste-water treatment plant.

"This is serious," she said. She looked serious, so I didn't make any more jokes.

"What happened?"

"He got bit."

"*Bit?*"

"On his leg. His calf."

"By who—Queenie?"

Mary smiled a little. Queenie was their ancient English bulldog. She was probably the only creature on earth who would even tolerate his company anymore—as long as she could have a good bite now and again.

"No . . . ," she answered, but she let it go.

"By who—or what?" I repeated.

She looked ahead strangely. I could see she'd like to change the subject.

"Actually, I'm not even supposed to talk about it," she finally said. "I just wanted you to know it was—you know—the real thing."

"A rat?" I asked. Some of those sewer rats were supposedly as big as cats.

She looked at me. The sun shone directly on her face, bleaching her hair and eyelashes even whiter, and showing the veins in her temple. She looked as though she was going to say yes, but she never lied to me. That was how I always knew she loved me. When it came down to anything, no matter what—even if she was trembling over something her father had forbade her to do, or discuss—she never lied to me.

"Something like that," she said.

"Well, what was it?" I couldn't help but smile. I couldn't imagine what.

"I'm not supposed to—" she began again.

"Come on, come on!"

"It's like a security thing—because of the Department of Public Works. . . ."

"Something bit him, and it's Top Secret?"

"Sort of confidential."

"Who would I tell?"

"If he ever found out—"

"He won't even talk to me—come on!"

But she still wouldn't say. We were on her street now.

"A squirrel—or something crazy? A raccoon?" I tried.

There was all kinds of color in her face now. "Tom," she said. She could always melt me, just by using my name.

"A snake?" Some pretty wild things got into the sewers, I'd been told. I'd read about a boa constrictor once that had crawled down into some sewer somewhere.

She looked at me as if I was close.

I could only come back to rats. I must have looked pretty pathetic, trying to guess. I was racking my brain. I hate mysteries, and Mary and I had never had any secrets. She'd told me everything, even down to the details of her mother's running off with the French teacher, five years before.

"Not a word to anyone," she said.

"You know me."

"Yes, I do. That's why I'm warning you . . ."

"Come on, come on."

"It's a little strange, I know," she said, smiling, and you could actually see that she was relieved now, to be telling someone.

"I'm ready for anything."

She paused a minute, right there on the sidewalk. Then she told me, in dead seriousness.

"An alligator."

"What?" I didn't think I'd heard right.

"An alligator," she repeated.

I started to laugh. "An *alligator?*"

"I know it sounds strange," she said as she started walking again. "But I guess there are some down there."

"Alligators? In the sewers?"

"In the old pipe sections," she said. "Not in the plant. Down under."

"*Alligators?*" I repeated, like a halfwit. "In the *pipes?*"

"I guess people flush them down the toilet," she said. "Pets from Florida. And they live off the sludge. In the warmer sections, anyway."

"Oh," I said. I could see that. "You mean little ones."

"I guess they're not always so little."

"You mean they get big? And breed?"

"I think there's a regular colony down there now," she answered. "At least in one of the old brick sections, from the thirties. I wasn't supposed to know, but I've heard my father discussing it with plant people on the phone. I guess it's getting to be a real problem. Now please—" she added, looking at me.

But I cut right in. "And one *bit* your father?"

"Yes! He was down there doing repairs."

"Came right out of the . . . water—and *bit* him?"

"He shot it," she said.

"He shot it?" I just kept on repeating. I couldn't believe it.

"He never goes down there without a shotgun," she added. "Maybe that's why he's got such a huge rifle collection."

I felt a little stunned. She never lied. If she said there were alligators, there were alligators. Or at least she believed it.

"Is it a deep bite?"

She shivered. "You should see his calf. Like hamburger. I guess they grind their jaws after they clamp down. . . ."

"Jesus Christ."

"Now you know why I've got to get home."

"Didn't the police—or the newspapers—"

"No one knows!" she interrupted. "And if anyone ever did . . ." She started to tremble. "If he finds out I told you . . ." She really was terrified, just like a child. "You know how he is about that place. Like it's all his."

"Okay, okay," I said. "Don't worry." But I was trembling myself.

And there was the house. That beautiful lot, with that horrible big board fence around it.

And—God. There was Mr. Malgren, standing out in front of his gate, baggy pants and a T-shirt, waiting.

"Oh . . . ," Mary said, with a little panic.

"Relax."

She stopped dead. "You'd better go back now. Thanks for walking me home."

"Okay." But her trembling was pitiful. It was as

though I were leaving her to face a monster. It got to me. So I did something funny. "Come on," I said, "I'll walk you to your gate." And started walking.

"Tom." She had to follow, or just stand there. "You promised!"

"Don't worry, I won't say a word. I'm just walking you home."

"Just say hello and go."

"Just hello and go," I repeated, walking. She was at my side again. I was grinning like a fool. I guess she was trying, too. And all the while, Old Man Malgren came closer and closer, just standing there by his board fence. Queenie was there too, with her vicious old sacks hanging down on each side, like a huge black scrotum.

"Hi, Mr. Malgren!" I said in my best broadcasting voice, the minute we were within earshot. While in my mind all I could hear was Cherry's big bass, reading:

> Dear Five-Star:
> Have I heard reports of alligators in the city's sewer system . . . ?

Three

He didn't answer. He just glared ominously. I'd never met anyone in my life who went more out of his way to be disagreeable. He hunched there, dark and hairy as a little ape, one hand on the gate. When Mary got close enough, he opened the gate for her. But he closed it the instant she was inside, as if I might try to scoot in behind her. Even when she bent to give him a little kiss on his cheek, that scowl never left his face, and his eyes never left mine. Queenie, standing beside him, looked just as malignant. I was glad for the board fence, which I could just see over. I think it irritated him that I was tall enough to do that. Mr. Malgren was a very short man, a head shorter than his own daughter.

"And how are you tonight, Mr. Malgren?" I asked loudly, so that he couldn't really walk away, at least not without a nod.

"Hungry," he grunted. Then he said to his daughter, "You're late."

"We got tied up in the Journalism Building," I said—still loudly and very genially, grinning up a storm. Queenie gave me a dirty look and began to salivate.

He still didn't really look at me. He seemed disgusted. I glanced at his legs. I could tell which one it was—the left—by the bulge—a bandage?—underneath the pants. And when he started walking away with Mary, the limp was very noticeable.

"Did you hurt your leg, Mr. Malgren?" I shouted.

He stopped. Mary turned around, her eyes big, but I just grinned at her, and grinned at him. His doleful old eyes searched mine, then hers, but I don't think he could read anything in either of our faces. Not in mine, for sure.

"I noticed you're limping," I said.

"What's it your business?"

"I just hope it's nothing serious. I'd hate to see you incapacitated."

"Inca—what?"

"Incapacitated," I repeated.

"Don't use seventy-five-cent words with me!" he said. Mr. Malgren hated eggheads—maybe because his wife had run off with one. He looked so ancient standing there, so finished. He wasn't that old a man, but there was something dead in him.

"What're you grinning at?" he asked, like a kid in the street who wants to fight. Queenie picked it right up and began to growl horribly, low in her throat. I had the terrible feeling suddenly that he was going to open that gate and sic her on me.

"I'm just happy," I answered. "We had the

greatest walk home—and it's a beautiful afternoon—and I just feel great!"

"Is that why you're late?" he asked, turning
around to his daughter. "I told you, I don't want
you running around!"

"She wasn't running around, Mr. Malgren. We
were working on our news feature."

"Don't tell me what you were doing!" he said
loudly. Queenie barked. "I know goddamn well
what you were doing! I know goddamn well what
all you college punks are doing!" Mary turned
very pale. He motioned to her. "Get in the
house." He turned back to me. "And you haul
your grinning ass out of here!" He put one hairy
hand on the gate, as if he might let the dog out.

"Okay, Mr. Malgren," I said, never letting up
on my smile. "Sorry if I bothered you. It isn't
Mary's fault she's late, though. It's mine. She was
helping us—"

"I don't want to hear your shit!" he said. He
turned around and began walking—limping—up
the path.

"Anyway," I called out, "I hope your leg gets
better!"

He stopped again, cold. He looked back. He
turned around and sort of squinted at me, maybe
trying to read through my words. But there really
wasn't that much behind them. I did feel sorry for
him, and I really did hope his leg would heal. I always wanted Old Man Malgren to like me. Always. For my sake, and for Mary's. I smiled again.

He turned around and walked back up the

path. The old dog hobbled behind him, turning a couple times to eye me. Queenie had a limp too— and warts and open sores and mange and all the other maladies of ancient dogs. Only, poor Queenie seemed to have them all at once.

I turned around and walked toward home. I walked slowly. It really was a beautiful neighborhood, and it really was a beautiful afternoon, and I really was happy, no matter what. That was the thing about Mary and me. No matter what, we really did love each other. But that was the rub, too, the thing that was always on my mind. If it came right down to it, who would she choose? If he said no, and I said yes? Me, I truly did believe, but I always wanted to know it, to see it, for sure.

I didn't regret the scene. Not really. All the way home I kept worrying about his laying into her, but if I'd had it to do over, I would have done the same thing. I wanted the old man to *accept* me. And he wouldn't. He just wouldn't. He wouldn't accept anything or anyone. He hated the world. Mary used to tell me that his favorite expression, whenever she would mention something good about the world, was "The world's fine, but people stink."

I didn't turn at the corner. I took the long route back. I just wanted to breathe. The air was so good out there. City University was all smog and noise, but that neighborhood was all freshness and color. You could smell mint. You could smell lilac. *The world's fine, but people stink.* And he worked in a sewer.

It was his wife, of course. Losing his wife. Mary had told me that a thousand times. And I could see it. Coming home and finding your wife in bed with the French tutor—Mr. Amour, yet! From what Mary had told me, her mother had been very beautiful. And bright—way out of the old man's league. Which Mr. Malgren must always have known, and which must have bothered him. It bothered him now that Mary was so beautiful, too. Just like her mother, in fact. And of course I was the new French teacher. And now, as she got older, everything Mary did was just like her mother. She was a tramp, like her mother. A liar, like her mother. Loose, like her mother. Sneaky, like her mother. Which of course wasn't even remotely close to anything like Mary—and which might not have been close to anything like her mother, either, if I was to go by what Mary had told me. Her mother was supposed to have been a small, light-hearted woman who went out of her way to cheer up her morose, alcoholic husband. And when that didn't work, she took to books and lessons. Which is where Mr. Amour came in, and which is where the old man came in, one night . . .

Mary had told me one story, though, that always sort of eased any ugly feelings I might have had about Mr. Malgren. She said that on the night of the big blowup, she had come home from high school to find her father on his hands and knees in her parents' bedroom, with a bucket and a scrub brush. The sheets were all off the bed, the curtains were down, the rugs were all rolled, the bureau drawers were all empty, and he was gasping—and scrubbing, with soap and water, trying to wash away every trace of sin. He never even looked up. He just told her in a husky voice, between pants, that her mother had left, that she wasn't coming back, and that if Mary wanted to live here, she'd better get used to making supper and doing the dishes, because they no longer had a mother to make supper and do dishes. Then the old man finished the floor, emptied the bucket, threw away the sheets—he wouldn't even launder them—and moved everything out of the room. He moved up to the guest room, where he'd been sleeping ever since. And Mary made dinner and did the dishes, which she'd been doing ever since.

I could always picture that scene somehow, and feel what he was feeling then—the total defeat—and so I always had a little sympathy for that homely, insecure little man after that, no matter how insulting he became.

*

Sympathy, but not surrender.

When I got back to the dorm, I called her. I knew Mr. Malgren would answer, so I put on my Betsy voice. I was a Theatre minor.

Three rings.

"Hello?" Mr. Malgren, food in his mouth.

"Hello. Is Mary there, please? This is Betsy Fox."

"She's eating."

"Oh—I'm terribly sorry. If it weren't so impor-tant, I'd never call. It's about her English exam."

Pause. Chomp chomp.

Ordinarily, he'd just hang up if he was going to hang up. But he was a sucker for that academic thing. He hated eggheads, but for some perverse reason he demanded that Mary bring home straight A's. He dropped the receiver with a bang. "Mary!"

I waited.

"Hello?"

"Hi! This is Betsy!"

"Hello, Betsy."

"Is the old bastard listening?"

"Yes, Betsy, and I've asked you not to call when we're eating."

"Is everything okay? Did he beat you?"

"No. It's fine."

"Say 'English exam.' "

"English exam."

" Good. Is he right behind you?"

"That's right."

"Listen! I've got an idea! Let's do the alligator story!"

There was a terrible pause. Nothing.

"Let's! Does he think he has the rights on the sewers or something? That's a fantastic story for *Touring.* Straight adventure! The Last Frontier!"

"No, Betsy."

"Freedom of the Press! Who does he think he is—Nixon?"

"I can't talk anymore, Betsy. I'll see you tomorrow."

"Wait a minute! Say Canterbury Tales.' Say it!"

There was a pause. "Canterbury Tales."

"Essay question. Say 'The essay question.' "

"The essay question."

"You know those brick things you were talking about? The old sewers or whatever? From the thirties? Where are they located?"

"I haven't the remotest idea, Betsy."

"Can you find out? He must have some kind of operations manual—maps or diagrams or something!"

"Good night, Betsy."

"The Rime of the Ancient Mariner."

"The Rime of the Ancient Mariner."

"Will you try to find out?"

"No."

"What if I give you a kiss and a hug?"

"Thanks for the call, Betsy."

"Even if we could just get a general idea. He'd never have to know you were involved. Besides, you're twenty-one!"

"Twenty."

"How about it?"

"Good night, Betsy."

"For me—do it?"

"See you tomorrow."

"I love you."

There was a pause. A long pause.

Then she said, "You, too."

Four

Alligators? In the *sewer*?"

Cherry howled—so loudly that her laugh carried right out over the campus lawns. We were outside by the fountain, on the grass—or what was left of the grass. It was Exchange, and lots of people were passing.

"Not too loud," I said. Hunk was with us, and Krevitch. We were having an emergency Five-Star production meeting. The only one absent was Mary, who would never cut a class.

"Where did you pick this up?" Cherry asked.

"Informed Sources."

"And it's true?"

"I think so." I looked around to test the others' reactions. Krevitch sat there in the sunlight, looking scared. He had a mustache of about fourteen hairs, which he always licked when he was nervous. His tongue was right up there now. Hunk wasn't really with us. He was stuffing a banana into his mouth. Only Cherry seemed to have the spirit. But then, Cherry and I were always the guiding lights of Five-Star.

"Inspired!" Cherry shouted, and rolled a little

on the lawn, laughing. A stranger might have thought she was having a fit, but most of the student body knew her by now. When she sat back up, there was a huge crushed area in the clover. She was all grass stains. "When do we go? Where? How?"

"I'm working on that," I said. "First, I just want to be sure we all agree." We always voted, since we usually had five different ideas. Four, actually; Hunk had no ideas at all.

"Sure," Cherry said. She raised one huge hand. Clover fell off her elbow.

I raised mine.

Krevitch looked doubtful. "I guess it would be a good wind-up for the year," he said. But he still had that timid look. And he didn't raise his hand.

"Hunk?" I asked. "What about you?"

"Huh?" He had a chocolate cupcake in his mouth. Maybe two.

"Yes or no?"

"Okay."

"That's three," Cherry said. We usually tried for at least four out of five.

"Mary votes no," I said. "She gave me her proxy."

"Why, for Christ's sake?" Cherry demanded. "It's the scoop of the year! *City News* will pick it up. Channel Two will pick it up. *Newsweek* will pick it up!"

"That's why—exactly."

"What do you mean?" She stared at me, with all that red frizz on her head looking even frizzier in the sun. I just let her stare a minute, and think. Her face was pockmarked and her lips were rubbery and her eyes were tiny and too close together, and once again I was amazed that any one person could have so many bad genes.

She couldn't make the connection. The fat on her jowls and arms actually quivered from the effort. She looked at Krevitch and Hunk, but they were no help at all. Krevitch was munching his mustache, and Hunk was now doing it to deviled eggs.

She looked back at me. Cherry and I were always in contest for the intellectual leadership of Five-Star.

"Whose father," I asked slowly, "is superintendent of the city waste-water plant?"

It dawned. Her face spread into a glorious acne-scarred grin showing lots of small brown teeth. "Ohhh . . . ," she said. "That's how you picked it up! That's right! The old man—he works in the sewer! Genius! Genius!" She whacked me on the shoulder, almost sending me over.

"Is he the guy," Krevitch asked, his voice cracking, "who always hangs up when we call Mary?"

"The same," I said.

"And who won't let us by the front fence, if we go over there?"

"That's the one."

"And who won't let Mary out past nine o'clock at night?" Krevitch continued.

"Seven," I said.

"And who telephones the press room if she's five minutes late?"

"Right. And who calls us all radicals."

"—And perverts!" Cherry added, lighting a cigarillo. She choked a little, and laughed.

Even Hunk made the association, to our amazement. "He's the one," Hunk said, with an enormous glob of strawberry jelly running down his face, "who called me a mongoloid."

"He's down on minorities," I said.

"He meant I was retarded," Hunk answered, staring at his strawberry jam sandwich.

"He thinks everyone is," I said. "He calls me a college punk." Everyone laughed, even Hunk, spraying jam everywhere.

"So what do we do if I vote yes?" Krevitch asked, the soul of caution. "Tour the treatment plant?"

"Naw," Cherry said. "There aren't any 'gators down there. I toured that dump a couple times in the Girl Scouts. It's like a fancy swimming pool, all brass and chemicals. You'd never find a fly in there."

"That's true," I said. "I've been over there with Mary once or twice. From the outside, it looks pretty sterile."

"We gotta go into a pipe, or something," Cherry said in perfect seriousness. Krevitch looked a little queasy again.

"—Or something," I said.

"I'll have to start getting the gear ready," Cherry began, completely on her own now, planning the expedition. Cherry was our commissary officer. She had an uncle in the Army surplus business, and she always came prepared. She had access to amazingly professional equipment.

"And I have to do a little preliminary research," I said.

"Hip boots," Cherry began, to herself. "Harpoons. Nets."

"It might all just be hearsay," Krevitch said.

"Flashlights," Cherry continued. "Gas masks. . . ."

"I don't know," I replied. "The thing that clued me into it was Mr. Malgren himself. He got bit by one."

Krevitch's tongue froze on his upper lip. "By an alligator?"

"That's what Mary said. And I saw the guy limping."

"He got attacked?" Krevitch's little voice hit a high and cracked in three. Hunk looked up from a peach. Even Cherry stopped.

"In the leg," I said. "He's home limping right now."

"First aid," Cherry continued. "Anti-tetanus. Tourniquet. Sutures. Gauze. . . ."

"So I suppose he's the man to check out first," I said. "No one would know more than he would."

"He called me retarded," Hunk said again, to his peach.

"A big one, or a little one?" Krevitch asked.

"Mary says a good-sized one," I answered. "By

the way, this is all classified Five-Star material. Not a word outside."

Krevitch swallowed. He had the most prominent adam's apple I'd ever seen on a human male. Or maybe it was the skinniest neck.

"Water-purifying pills," Cherry added. "Wax-coated matches. Crowbar. . . ."

"If there's any special location, he'd have the answer," I said. "No one else. He runs the whole show."

"He meant mental," Hunk said to the peach pit.

"Food, of course. Plastic bags. Canteen. Knives. . . ."

Even Krevitch was off into himself now, licking his entire upper face, and just thinking. It was amazing how all the members of Five-Star were basically loners. Krevitch sat there trembling like a caged mouse. He couldn't have weighed over a hundred pounds, but he'd always wanted to be a college jock—a football player. This is where he'd ended up.

Krevitch finally spoke, after picking a whisker off his tongue. "He'll never talk to you," he said. "Malgren."

"That's what you said about Wanda," I said. "Remember?"

"Who's Wanda?"

"The witch—the one with the dead chickens!"

Krevitch blanched, remembering.

"And Irene the hooker! She ended up giving us the whole red-light tour. Remember? And the Pigeon Lady. And the factory foreman, for 'What's in Your Soup?' People are always willing to talk, if you ask them the right way. They love to talk."

"Rope," Cherry said. "I suppose we'll need rope. . . ."

"I'm not retarded," Hunk said, sucking the peach pit. "I'm Exceptional. That's different."

Krevitch finally raised his skinny little arm to vote yes. I guess he thought we'd all been waiting. No one even looked but me.

"Good," I said. "Then it's all settled. Maybe Mary will swing over, too. If not, I hope at least she'll make the sandwiches."

"But we can't just jump in," Krevitch added. "We've got to know exactly what we're doing."

"That's where Mr. Malgren comes in," I said. "Hunk—are you eating that peach pit?"

Hunk stopped crunching a moment. Drool ran down both cheeks, with little pebbles of peach pit. "I like them," he said.

"Spit it out!"

He shook his head no. He swallowed. He coughed. He grinned. "I eat them all the time," he said. "They're good for you."

"A raft!" Cherry said. "What do you think? Could we use an inflatable raft?"

Five

It was still light. I waited until after seven, when I knew they'd be done eating. Mary had told me a hundred times that Friday was his bad drinking night. For hours after dinner he'd sit in front of the television, sipping beer. Something about weekends always made him maudlin, it seemed. Maybe the memory of better ones.

The gate was locked as always. There were lights on in the back of the house, in the kitchen. Mary didn't know I was coming. I did that purposely. She'd be honestly surprised, and he'd know it wasn't a set-up.

There was a little bell button just outside the gate. I was about to ring when I heard a clipping sound—the hard, quick snap of shears. I tiptoed up to look. There he was, way in back, trimming a portion of the high glossy hedge that completely surrounded the house. He was short and had to strain to reach the top foliage. He was snapping that clipper and grunting, then reaching even higher, with a little jump, and snapping again. Queenie was lying right there, peppered with debris, but the old girl was probably too senile to sense me.

I waited a second to get my nerve. The proverbial beers were all there, lined up one after the other on the edge of the picnic table.

I cleared my throat.

"Hello, Mr. Malgren! How are you tonight?"

Queenie exploded slowly. She lumbered up, tripped, barked, growled and then plunged across the lawn to the gate. She hit it with everything she had. The gate strained, but it held. The poor old beast was snorting and slobbering and choking and dripping, and on top of that she'd ripped her ear open on something. She should have been destroyed years earlier.

"Hello, Queenie, old girl," I added. "How's the world treating you?"

She just kept lunging and barking—hoarsely, gasping for breath.

Mr. Malgren began that slow, familiar walk of his, holding those shears. He looked even worse in the sunset, like a little troll that had crawled out from hiding. And he was still limping badly.

When he finally had Queenie off the gate, he looked at me and said, "Mary's not going out." That was all.

Then he turned and walked away.

"I didn't come to see Mary," I called. "I came to see you." I smiled, even though he wasn't looking.

He stopped. He stood still, with his back to me. Probably no one had said that to him in years. He turned around. I gave him an even bigger smile, the one I used all during the Student Council election.

"About what?" he asked.

"I need some help, Mr. Malgren." I held up the books I had under my arm, so he could see. *Sewage Purification and Disposal*, by Kershaw. *The Ecology of Waste-Water Treatment*, by Hawkes. And *Sewers for Growing America*, by Morris M. Cohn. "I've got to do a report on waste-water treatment, and I just don't know where to begin."

"You never will, either," he answered, and turned back around to his bushes. But he didn't go all the way back. He started trimming closer to the gate, which meant I had _him_ curious, anyway.

"I knew you were the only one who could come up with the answers," I called loudly, with real enthusiasm. "These books are worthless to me." His ears perked up a little on that one. So I repeated, "Absolutely worthless!"

"That's what I been telling you for years," he said, shearing away at the hedge. Brush covered his small feet.

"And you've been right, Mr. Malgren. I should have listened to you all along. It's not college that counts. It's experience! The real thing!" I was still shouting.

"You college punks always think you got all the answers," he said to the leaves.

"Until we run into real problems!" I continued. "Then we find out fast enough!"

Clip! He took out a huge section—and not too evenly, either. "Using those goddamn seventy-five-cent words all the time," he said. He was clipping furiously now to get that patch even. It got worse and worse. When he glanced at me, I pretended not to notice.

"You've sure got that even, Mr. Malgren." It was like talking to a kid. No. A kid would have seen through it. "Right down to the inch," I added.

"To the millimeter," he said, taking off another six inches.

"That's right! We're into metrics now. Of course that's not new to you. Engineers have always used the metric system, haven't they? That's one thing about us in the everyday world, isn't it, Mr. Malgren? We're always a little behind the world of science." I had to be careful there with those engineering references, because Mary had told me he didn't have a degree in Sanitary Engineering. He'd learned what he'd learned in the Navy.

"I don't have time to stand here and bullshit," he said. He started to walk away from that horrible chunk he'd taken out of the shrubbery.

"Mr. Malgren," I shouted, "what's a *polysaprobic condition*—in a sludge bed?" I read it off a piece of notepaper tucked inside one of the books.

He turned around. "What?"

"A polysaprobic condition," I repeated. "You know—in a sludge bed?"

He looked at me with that old disgust. "You don't know your ass from left field," he said, "standing there talking about sludge beds."

"I know, I know," I said. "That's why I'm here! To ask a pro!" I could hardly keep my face muscles from twitching. But something happened just then, with that last word. Every man must want to be a pro. Suddenly you could catch the slightest change in him. He picked up a huge pile of trimmings with both hands and began to stuff them into the can, but without any of the impatience of earlier. He did it very carefully, almost gently. And when the can was full, he began to carry it towards the gate.

Where I was.

The fates must have been with me. The garbage-can rack was outside the gate.

He unlocked it while I was standing there. Queenie lunged, but he just sort of kicked her down. He still didn't look at me as he lugged the can out and heaved it up onto the stand. But he didn't elbow me out of the way, either. He took down another empty to bring inside. When he passed back through the gate, he didn't shut it.

Even Queenie looked amazed.

I walked right in. I shut the gate behind me.

The old guy knew I was there. He still wouldn't look at me, but he wouldn't not look at me, either. He was all sweat and smelled rank, but something about him had changed. Queenie knew it, too. I smiled at Queenie. I smiled at Mr. Malgren's sweaty back. I smiled at the garbage can. I looked up and saw Mary's surprised face in the window, and I smiled at her, too. She looked shocked—scared. But I just kept smiling.

"*Heterotrophic bacteria,* too," I said, flashing my notes again. "And *microbial flocs.* They're really throwing them at me!"

The light was getting bad now. There were trimmings all up and down the hedge—piles and piles. I didn't even ask him. I just went and got another can, and started stuffing. "You know," I said, talking to Queenie and to the shadows and to the piles of huge trimmings and to Mr. Malgren's baggy pants, "the trouble with growing up is that sometimes you just don't know what you don't *know*—you know?"

He stopped stuffing a second, as though he was trying to figure that one out. Then he started grunting again. You could smell the beer off him, too—beer and sweat, like a downtown bar. He had his can full. I had to hurry with mine. There weren't any more cans, and there wasn't that much more rubbish, either—at least, not on the ground.

"You know," I continued, "every time I come over here, I can see the engineering expertise. I can see it in the whole house—the way you built that fence—and the locks on the doors—and those window bars. You're an expert. You've got everything just so."

"You got to," he said. "The niggers'll get in."

"And you've done it all yourself—because you're technically adept." I almost blew it there, with that seventy-five-cent word, but he picked it right up.

"They'll rob you blind if you try to get it done on the outside."

"I know," I said. "A man can't even afford to have his toilet back up anymore. Plumbers make more than doctors."

"They don't make more than me."

"That's right! You're a superintendent!"

"*The* super. There's only one."

"That's right! And I know you make good wages."

"Top wage," he said. "We just got a new union contract. Top wage in the city."

"More than I'll make as newspaperman."

"Bet your ass on that!"

"Which is why I've been seriously considering taking up Waste-Water Treatment as a career, Mr. Malgren. Which is why I'm here tonight. I want to grow."

He looked up at me. Maybe that wasn't the best word to use, with my height and all. I plowed right on through.

"And I want to alert the student body over there to the facts of life, too," I added.

"That's right. You gotta have water."

"You sure do. People should return to basics."

"And forget all this welfare shit," he said.

"For sure."

He looked up as though he might be thinking, or trying to. Or maybe he was just checking the light. He rubbed his chin, and his whiskers crackled. I jammed on the top of my garbage can.

"Not too tight," he said, "or the bastards can't get it off."

"Sorry." I loosened it.

"Then they throw the can all over the driveway. Look at the dents! And do you know what they make? Garbage men?"

"A lot, I know."

"Too much. They're robbing the city blind."

We each hauled a can out to the racks. It was definitely dark now.

"*Saprophytic fungi*, too," I said. "That's another sticky one."

He blanked. He just looked at me.

"Saprophytic fungi?" I repeated.

"I ain't no goddamn teacher," he exploded with real loathing. All I could think of was the French tutor, Mr. Amour.

I fielded it. "Good, because teachers are my whole problem. I can't stand them. They're worthless. That's why I came to you—to a real man on the job!"

He went over and washed his hands at the faucet on the side of the house. I stood right behind him.

Finally he said, "I got a couple plant manuals in the house. They ain't that library crap you're reading, but they got diagrams—"

"That's just what I was hoping for!" I said immediately. "Diagrams!"

"I only got a couple minutes," he added. "At eight o'clock I watch the fights."

"A couple minutes would be great," I said. "A

couple minutes will change the direction of my whole life!"

"Cut the philosophy crap," he said. He couldn't get his key to work in the door. Maybe it was the beer. He gave the door a smash, then a kick.

"Mary!" he finally shouted. "Open the goddamn door!"

Six

He really was drunk. I hadn't noticed it so much outside, but once we were in the house, it was obvious. He was bumping into things, he was weaving, and he was slurring.

"Mary," he said, not even looking at her, "bring me a beer."

He set two manuals down on the kitchen table, next to my books. They were old and well thumbed and dirty.

Then he collapsed into the chair next to me.

Mary brought two beers. "Tom, would you like one?" she asked.

"No," her father answered for me. "He won't be here that long." Drunk or not, he never lost his ugly touch.

Mary returned the one beer to the refrigerator.

He started leafing through the larger of the two books. I glanced up at Mary, but then I looked away quickly. I didn't want to meet those eyes of hers. I didn't want anything to undercut my determination.

"It's all here," Malgren said when he'd found the place. But then he took a swig of beer, and the pages flipped, and he had to start all over again. I remained as quiet as possible, praying he wouldn't sober up suddenly and smarten up. I'd never been inside this house before. Never, not in the three years I'd known Mary. Yet it all seemed very familiar, because of the hundreds of times she'd talked about the things that had happened here. I knew this kitchen and I knew the living room—the gun rack, the fireplace—and I even guessed that right up those stairs, just off the living room, was the legendary master bedroom of the big scene five years earlier. . . .

He found his spot again. I almost groaned. It was a big colored diagram, exactly like the one I remembered from high school. Or maybe grade school. There was the Influent Pipe, followed by the Main Settling Tanks. Primary, Secondary, Tertiary. The Solid Skimmer. Grit Filter. Aeration Tank, Sand Filter. Chlorination Tank . . . none of which had anything to do with reptiles in the pipes.

"Now," Mr. Malgren said, with a beery sigh, "this here's the standard set-up. I don't know about all those fancy words you got on that piece of paper, but if you know this you know water treatment." He took another swig of beer. "Raw sewage pipes into these three settling tanks," he began. "One, two, three. . . ."

And away he went. I *did* remember it all suddenly, exactly as Cherry had earlier. Not from Girl Scouts, but close—grade school Science I. Sixth or seventh grade. A field trip. I could still see Mr. Rodriguez leading us through those smelly cement rooms. Mr. Malgren must have been there too, on the job, ten years before, while I was running around with jujubes stuck in my teeth. Amazing. . . . I yawned.

"Now you got that?" he asked. "What the skimmer does?"

"Skims off the solid wastes," I repeated.

"Ain't you gonna take notes?" he asked. "What if they test you?"

"I try to keep it all in my head."

So he took off again, belching. "Once it's skimmed and cleared the Grit Tank, you gotta emulsify the suspended particles. That's where this comes in. . . ." He pointed to another tank and I nodded, all the while trying to see under his elbow, where the smaller book, a kind of binder, was pinned. There was a sort of tissue centerfold, half in and half out. A diagram—maybe—of the plant's underground system? I was willing to bet. Maybe the pipes for the whole city. It was an enormous folded piece. The more he jiggled his arm, the more that centerfold buckled, until I could actually see all the little lines and networks and squares and circles, like a fine architect's drawing. And small—very tiny—labels. *Storm tunnel,* I read. *Conduit A. Conduit B.* A scale indicator, and little route arrows. . . .

"This thing looks just like a big merry-go-round," he said. He laughed a little, pleased with his own line. "Once the water goes through this, it's pure enough to drink. You might not believe it, but it is."

"Sand Filter," I read, so that he'd stop pointing. His fingertip was black and very chewed up, as though he'd mashed it in quite a few pipes in his time.

"You know what chlorination is, don't you?" he asked.

"Yes," I answered, but he started in anyway. That's when I took the flyer.

"Mr. Malgren," I interrupted.

"Huh?" He was right in the middle of bubbling the chlorine gas through the emulsified solution.

"Is there a section of the sewer from the thirties—an old brick section—that's not in use anymore?"

He just stared. Mary was making panic motions behind him, but I didn't look at her. Then Mr. Malgren was staring hard at me, and the glaze cleared for a moment.

"Who told you that?" he asked.

"I remember it from grade school Science. Mr. Rodriguez took us all down there once."

"In the sewers?"

"Not right in them, but over to the plant. And he told us that there were new sewers and old sewers."

"Well, sure, you got old sewers down there."

"Made out of bricks?" I repeated.

"Yeah, that's what they made them out of. . . ." He definitely was uncomfortable, and avoiding my eyes.

"Does anything . . . is there anything in them?"

"What do you mean—anything?" he asked. Mary was rolling her eyes now, so I had to go easy.

"Water or anything," I said.

"Of course there's water. They're still used for storm runoff."

"But not for regular sewage."

"No. We got all concrete and asbestos now. Who needs bricks?"

"They're just sort of down there?"

"Where the hell else would they be—up in the air?"

"Are they all over the city—or what?"

He looked at me very impatiently. "There's only one section," he said. "That's all the city there used to be in the thirties. Why the hell all these questions on the Catacombs?"

"The Catacombs?"

"That's what we call them." And he laughed.

I laughed, too. "I was just interested in—you know—the History of Sewers."

"They ask you that stuff, too?"

"Everything," I said. "You'd be surprised. What's that?" I pointed to the second book, the binder, glad that I had him conversing.

"The Plant Operations Manual."

"May I see?"

"*No.*" He clutched the thing strangely. He looked at me a little more sharply, too, alcohol and all. "This is classified."

"Classified?"

"It's got the city's whole pipeline system charted out."

"And that's classified?"

"You bet! What if some radical bastards wanted to bomb the pipes? They'd know just where to go in."

"Oh," I said. I looked at Mary. She was moving her head *no*. I glanced back at Mr. Malgren. He was cradling his little manual as if it were a baby.

I got bold. "What happened to your leg, Mr. Malgren?"

"What?"

"I noticed you're still limping."

He looked down at his leg. "I hurt it."

"At work?"

"I—" He stopped. He looked at me, but I just smiled. "Yes," he said.

"How?"

He wasn't used to being questioned. I think I surprised him. He didn't know how to parry. "How? I—I got—I cut it."

"On a pipe?"

"Yeah. Something like that."

"I thought maybe something bit you."

"What?" He turned right around and looked at Mary.

"Like a rat or something," I continued in my most innocent voice. "I've heard there are some crazy things down there.

"You got rats everywhere," he said.

"But I've heard they get as big as cats down there."

"You hear too much," he said. He stood up. The lesson was over. "Don't believe everything you hear."

I had to gather my books and stand up, too. "I just hope your leg's all right," I said, sort of sinking as he scooped up his little black manual.

"My leg's fine."

"I suppose you'll be out of work for a while."

All the old disgust and anger came back into his face. "Out of work! What the hell you talking about? Who would hold the place together? The first storm and the whole city would back up!" His voice went very high, and he was turning another color completely. He breathed beer on me. And there was something else too, just then. He caught me glancing down at the small manual in his hand, and a definite expression came into his eyes, right through the alcoholic haze. It was more than suspicion, more than dislike, more even than hate. It was fear. He was afraid of something.

I'd never seen that look on him before.

"Well, thanks a lot, Mr. Malgren," I said, "for all your time. I really appreciate it." I held out my hand, but he wouldn't take it.

"I'm late for my fight," he said, and walked right out of the kitchen with his manual, into the living room.

Then the television came on, loud.

*

Mary walked me to the gate.

"Idiot," she said. "What are you trying to do?"

"Did you see his eyes?"

"I've seen his eyes for twenty years."

"I mean when I asked about the—what did he call them—the Catacombs. Why is he trying to cover up the alligators?"

"Forget the alligators!" she said, so vehemently that I had to look. I'd never seen her that passionate. I'd never seen her that excited. She'd never even raised her voice to me before. I kind of liked it. I smiled. I gave her a big hug. Then a kiss. A good one.

But when I let her go, she was still keyed up. Of course, I made it worse. "Can you sneak me out that manual?" I asked.

"Absolutely not."

"Just the centerfold part?"

"Forget it."

"I want to get a route to those Catacombs."

"You're insane. You're trying to get me killed."

"Just for a day?"

"No."

"For a couple hours, then?"

"Good night."

"Weren't you kind of surprised to see me tonight?"

"Yes."

"Were you glad?"

"No."

"Just a little?"

"No," she repeated. But then she made the mistake of looking at me, and she had to smile slightly. "Yes," she said.

I gave her another kiss. "1 sure would like that manual."

"See you tomorrow," she answered.

I tickled her a little. "With the manual?"

"Good night," she said. She ran back up the driveway.

"Good night!" I called, but she didn't look back. She just opened the door and went inside the house.

Seven

The only dates we ever had off campus were sneakies—like meeting her when she did her shopping. Saturday was the supermarket. I found her by the fish sticks.

"I've only got a half-hour," she said. "He wants me home before he goes to Union Hall." She had her hair up, very old-fashioned. She was wearing a dress, too. She knew I liked her in dresses.

"Did you smuggle the book out?" I asked.

"Do you want me murdered?" She said it so seriously that I didn't press. But I did start trying to figure out another way—immediately—like getting over there today, while he was at Union Hall.

"Push the cart," she said. I did. She already had a load. Four six-packs of beer.

"Did you bring the car?" I asked.

"Of course." She dumped in three half-gallons of ice cream, the crappy stuff, all chemicals—maple nut.

"He sure does eat the junk, doesn't he?"

"He sure does," she answered, but without bitterness. Just that old resignation, as if she were caring for an invalid. And as we went up and

49

down the aisles, she loaded on even more junk food—jelly, cookies, lunch meat, gigantic Hershey bars. a frozen cream cake. . . . Then she put in a bunch of bananas.

"That's for you," she said "I'll put all your stuff on this side." She put in a half-gallon of milk for me, too. And a chunk of cheese—Oshkosh sharp, my favorite brand. "You can keep this on the dorm windowsill," she said. "Eat it! You're getting too skinny."

"When he got bit," I said, "where exactly did he say it was?"

"On the calf—I told you."

"I mean, where in the sewers."

"Somewhere down in that old section."

"I mean, inside a pipe or a storm tunnel or a tank—or what?"

"One thing you have," she said. "Tenacity."

"I have to, to get you." I pinched her on the seat, by the lettuce.

"Cut it out. That old lady's watching."

I looked. Sure enough. Amazing. She looked just like Mr. Malgren, in drag. For a second I had the craziest sensation that maybe he was following us, disguised.

"Do you think he was right inside a pipe? In a little boat or something?" I continued.

"I don't think the water's that deep," she said.

"But you think he was inside the pipe—maybe wading?"

She stopped the cart. "No. Come to think of it, he said it was on a ledge."

"On a ledge? Like a pool or something?"

"That's what I was wondering. Maybe they have some old cisterns or holding tanks down there. I need coffee." She turned down the coffee lane. I had to maneuver that loaded cart—with one bum wheel, of course. I ran into the old lady again, who was still looking shocked. It definitely wasn't Mr. Malgren.

Coffee was up to a hundred dollars a pound, but Mary still bought two jars. Instant, decaffeinated.

"Does he have a hard time sleeping?"

"He has a hard time with everything," she said.

"So all we have to figure out is where the Catacombs actually are, and how to get down to them. I figured something out last night in bed," I began.

"Is that what you do all night—lie awake chasing alligators?"

"It is right now—because I haven't got anything better to chase!" I pinched her on her other side. She screamed and jumped—right into the dog food. Where that old lady was stocking up.

"I'm going to report you two to the manager!" the old lady shouted, holding a can of Gravy 'n' Gizzards.

We got out of there.

"Heat," I said. "They'd need heat to survive. There's no sun down there, right? And they can't function at under—I'd say—seventy degrees. So they'd naturally gravitate toward some warmer area. Which means the plant. Or under the plant maybe? The boiler room or something? Steam pipes?"

"Those gas traps," she said. "The methane pipes, the ones they light outside the plant to burn off the excess. They throw off a lot of heat."

"Even down below?"

"I think so. It's the fermentation of the sludge or something. Plus the sludge ovens themselves. It's like a brewery. There's lots of heat down there—I know. I've seen my father come home blistered a couple times."

"So you see? They get in from the houses. They work themselves down through the pipes—maybe even for months, eating off the sewage. Then they end up by the heat."

"Tea," she said. "I need tea."

"The one thing that amazes me," I continued, when I'd caught up with her, "is that they can see, after so many years down there in the dark."

"I don't think it's all that pitch black," she said. "They have generators going all the time, and light bulbs. I know, because whole sections of them are always blowing out, and they call my father."

"But I've read about the ones in New York being blind. Blind albinos—unless that's just a joke."

"I need hot Italian sausage," she said. "This is all mild. He won't eat anything but hot." She looked around hopelessly. It was amazing how wrapped up she could get in hot Italian sausage.

I rang the Meat Service Department.

"If I get the hot sausage, will you let me into the house this afternoon to get the book?"

"He takes it to the meeting with him," she answered. She smiled sort of strangely, as if enjoying my efforts.

The butcher appeared in his refrigerator-box window.

"Do you have any hot Italian sausage back there?" I asked. "This is all mild."

He surprised us. He had it.

"You're wonderful," she said to me, when it was safely in the cart. "Mustard. Come on." And away we went. She was terribly disorganized. She got things as she thought of them. We ran into the old lady again, by the olives. She looked terrified.

"She probably needs a good pinch," I said. I walked toward her.

"Tom!"

The old lady ran, pulling her cart.

I laughed.

"Behave yourself!"

"What's the least busy working day over there?" I asked. "When do they have the lightest crew on?"

"Today," she said. "Saturdays. Weekends, but Saturdays especially, because that's when they run those tours for community groups."

"Which means the engineers all stay upstairs?"

"The ones they have. I don't think there's more than three or four over there anymore. They only bring more in for emergency repairs."

"Your father made it sound like there were lots of emergency repairs."

She just shook her head. "It's pretty dull in a sewer." She put a big jar of peanut butter in, on my side. "That's all protein," she said. "Make yourself a big sandwich every night. Really, all you do is think. You're getting too thin."

"I need some tender loving care."

"Here's what you need," she said, and took a couple of folded sheets out of her purse.

At first I didn't get it. I wasn't ready for it. I couldn't believe it. I just stared at the sheets. That was it. Photocopies of the tissue centerfold. She hadn't been able to fit the whole thing on, so she'd copied it in sections. But it was all there. She'd done it.

For me.

"I think the brick section is right here," she said, and pointed to something neatly labeled *Storm Conduit*. They even had the little brickwork arches delineated.

"How . . . ?" I just couldn't believe it.

"He fell asleep during the first round," she said. "Like always. I took it off his lap and ran it down to the corner."

I tried to think. On the corner was one of those all-night-everything stores, called Seven-Eleven.

"Oh, Thank Heaven," she said, "for Seven-Eleven!" She started laughing a little, then a lot. It was the first time I'd seen her laugh in a long time. She had the world's most beautiful teeth. It was like a whole new thing opening up. I grabbed her and hoisted her high, by the low-fat milk.

"Put me down!" she cried, laughing, just as the manager appeared, flanked by the little old lady.

'There!" the old lady said. "See? In a public place!"

The manager looked a little confused, as though he'd expected to find us on the floor. Mary and I both grabbed the three-legged cart, laughing, and split down the aisle.

"Let's check this stuff out and get out of here," she said, heading for the front of the store. She paid for it all—even mine—with her father's check.

Eight

We took the journalism staff car, a big long yellow hearse. It was a donation to the University's Communications Department from our local Avant Mortuary—for tax purposes, probably. All it took was a new paint job and a few major repairs and we had the perfect vehicle for Five-Star expeditions.

"Are you sure it's on Badian Avenue?" Cherry asked. She was wearing her Army combat outfit, and driving. She had the terrible habit of turning her head around completely while at the wheel, staring at all of us from behind her aviation sunglasses.

"Watch out—a truck!" Krevitch screamed. He was up front with her.

"Relax! Relax!" she said, swerving. The hearse was so long that the back whiplashed, and the rest of us flew. You could actually feel the frame strain. "I grew up out here," Cherry continued, without a pause. "Badian and 28th. I got raped out here a couple times, but I sure don't remember any kind of sewer building. Just the junk yard."

When I was upright, I checked my photocopy again. "I'm not sure it's a building. There's only a square here. It might be just a hatch or something. A point of entry."

She swerved again, just missing another hearse—a real hearse. She laughed uproariously. "Look!" she said, pointing to the black Cadillac. "A relative!"

Hunk was between us, trying to crawl out from under some of the equipment, which had shifted. "You okay, Hunk?"

He didn't answer. He just struggled with a tarp. But Hunk was always okay.

Mary and I were way in back, in the casket compartment. She was sort of quiet. She probably never would have come, except for our lunch. The mother instinct again. There was no one else in Five-Star who could make a sandwich the way Mary could. So she threw in.

"Cheer up," I said.

"No matter what," she answered, "I have to be home by three."

"We'll be home by three."

Cherry made another insane turn. Everything rolled right, including little Krevitch. "You're going to smash my camera!" he shouted. Cherry never heard him at all. Her color was high and her red afro was all combed out and she really was in all her glory.

"Slow down a little, Cherry," I said. "You know how they love to ticket hearses."

She roared, and gave it the gas. "We must be

pretty close now," she said. "There's the treatment plant!"

She was right. There it was, on our left, way across an open field. There was the cyclone fence, and the bright white tanks and domes, with the cement settling sections like so many swimming pools, side by side, end to end. You could also catch a change in the air—that old, familiar metallic sewer smell, reminding me of fishing worms that die and rot at the very bottom of the can.

"It's out further," I said, studying my sheets. "Keep going."

As we rolled by the plant, Mary froze up a little, as if her father might be right there, in that little check booth by the gate with the big sign: RESTRICTED. ALL VISITORS OBTAIN PASS FROM GUARD.

And he might have been, from the way he ran things.

"Did you bring your pass?" I asked Mary.

She didn't laugh.

"What are those torches?" Hunk asked.

"They're burning off excess methane," I answered. He looked puzzled. "Gas," I added. "You know, from the . . . sewage. So it doesn't explode."

He craned his big head back, toward the gigantic, rusty cylinders belching orange flames on two sides of the building. He looked exactly like a little kid yearning to see more.

"It looks just like torches," he repeated. "Like in the movies. . . ." Even when we were a good distance away, he was still gazing back at the plant. Mary and I glanced at each other a bit doubtfully. Hunk wasn't a student at the University. We'd run across him mowing the campus lawns one day, when we were hauling gear for the soup factory tour. He'd offered to help us tote, and he'd been with us on every expedition ever since. Sometimes we wondered if we wern't a little off-base with Hunk, because of his condition. But he was a great porter, and he loved it.

"We're pretty close now," Cherry said. "28th's coming up. Start looking."

There was nothing to see. Just open field— weeds and wildflowers. In the distance was a huge auto-wrecking plant and a dump yard, but none of it looked remotely like any kind of municipal works project. It seemed funny to see the twin signposts, Badian Ave. and 28th St., marking nothing. But Cherry pulled the big hearse over anyway. We skidded to a halt on the gravel shoulder of the highway.

It seemed very quiet. There wasn't even much traffic on the highway for a Saturday morning.

We all got out. It was almost eerie—the quiet. All we could hear was the occasional rush of a car behind us, and the wind in the weeds. A few birds were flying. The sun suddenly seemed very hot.

Mary began to pick wildflowers. 'Queen Anne's lace," she said. "I love it. I haven't seen any in years." But her voice sounded strange out here, too—tiny and whispery. I think all of us felt a little dwarfed, even big Cherry.

Or maybe we just hadn't been outside in a while.

"So what now?" Cherry asked, losing a little of her military bearing.

I checked my diagram again. "Badian and 28th," I said. "It's supposed to be right here."

"What's suppose to be right here?" Krevitch asked, swinging at a hornet hysterically.

"I don't know. Maybe some kind of cement pill-box or something?"

Everyone looked at me, even Hunk.

I gazed off into the field. "Come on," I said. "Let's take a look." We all tromped down the shoulder and into a ditch. Then up the side of the ditch, into the grass. We let Hunk plow the way. He was head and shoulders over the weeds—and just about as wide, too. He smashed a path through the thistles and milkweed and ragweed. We wandered around for maybe three minutes, sneezing and coughing, brushing away grasshop-pers—ripped, slashed, pricked, stung, bitten, cov-ered with burrs and nettles. Nothing. Then Hunk started to smash at his own face and head wildly, and there was the terrific shrieking of a bird. A starling was dive-bombing his head.

"There's a nest or something!" Krevitch yelled.

The starling hit. It actually drew blood on the very top of poor Hunk's head. Cherry drew her bayonet and started flailing.

"Leave it alone!" Mary shouted. "She's protect-ing her babies! Come on—let's go back."

We all trooped back through the weeds, toward the car, with the starling still screaming.

"Crows mean death," Krevitch said.

"That was a starling," I answered. We made it out of the ditch and back up to the car. It was amazing, though. Really amazing. Three minutes, and we were all standing there completely defeated—perspiring, itchy, exhausted and confused. City folk in a country field.

The cool breeze was a relief.

Cars came by. Drivers stared—at the yellow hearse or at us, we didn't know.

Cherry was looking down the highway. She took a swig of water out of her shoulder canteen, and then she stared some more. And some more. Then she shouted, "I've got it!"

"Where?" I asked. "What?"

Everyone looked at her—even Mary, who was already back in the car, maybe believing we really were going back.

"I've got it!" Cherry said again, laughing in the wind. "I figured it out!"

"What?" I said again. "Tell us!"

She just grinned. Her face was livid, sweaty, and all those tiny teeth looked even browner in the sunlight. "You guys," she said, "would never make it in a combat situation. Never!" Hunk felt the top of his bloody head.

Cherry laughed and did a little jig. "It's so obvious! Hahaha!" She rolled. She rocked. Cars really did slow down then. She was waving; she was running. She even got the hiccups. "We're all running around the field and it's right in front of our eyes!"

In front of our eyes? We all looked. We let our eyes travel up and down the road. . . .

There was the yellow hearse, and the field.

The signposts.

The dump.

The auto-wrecking plant.

And a train, whistling far off somewhere. . . .

"Think!" Cherry demanded. "When you were kids, how did you get down into the sewer?"

"We never went down into the sewer," I said.

"But you saw people go down, didn't you?" I had to think. We all had to think. We just stood around, thinking. And I guess we all got it about the same time, our eyes traveling down the road.

There was a manhole, a big, black, iron-grating-covered manhole, right beside the road.

"Hahaha!" Cherry roared again, strutting over to it. "There it is, boys!" She put one large foot on top of it, like Columbus planting his flag on the New World.

"Are you sure?" I asked.

"I don't think so . . . ," Krevitch said.

"No," Mary added.

Hunk was silent.

But I think we all knew she was right.

"Hunk," Cherry said, "the crowbar, if you please!"

Nine

Hunk pleased. He was always glad to be useful. He lumbered over to the hearse, opened up the rear end, and rifled through the bales and sacks and packs and boxes until he found the crowbar. He came running back with it, wearing the proudest look.

"Stand clear, men!" Cherry shouted. She looked up and down the highway to see if anyone was coming. There was no one out there at all. She jammed one point of the crowbar down into a section of the grating, like a pro. She gave a lunge, then a gasp.

Nothing.

"Locked," Krevitch said.

"They never lock these things," she answered. "They keep them open for emergencies." She lunged forward again, putting all two hundred pounds-plus down on the crowbar.

Nothing, again.

"They never used to, anyway," she said, gasping.

Krevitch came forward. He studied it; he tapped it. He took the crowbar and worked it under the rim on all sides. We all stood by respectfully. This was Krevitch's forté. Mary made sandwiches and Hunk toted and Cherry was quartermaster supreme, but Krevitch could go one better. He could crack any lock on anything at any time. We had an old saying in Five-Star: If Hunk couldn't kick it, Krevitch would pick it.

But he seemed puzzled too. His mustache twitched.

"It looks rusted," he said. "I don't think anyone has opened it in a while."

"You see?" Cherry said in triumph. "It's just rusted down. Come on!"

"Come on what?" I asked.

"Everyone!" she shouted. "On the crowbar! Let's go! On the count of three!"

We all got on it, with Hunk and Cherry almost covering the thing. Krevitch, Mary and I put our hands on their backs, poised, ready to throw on our weight.

"*One*," she called.

"*Two!*"

"*Three!*"

We all lunged—almost a thousand pounds on that crowbar. There was a wild moment when we all seemed suspended on the bending bar. Then there was a slight give, then more, and then the iron cap slipped and the crowbar slipped and we all slipped—into a pile.

"It's loose! It's loose!" Cherry screamed from underneath our struggling bodies. She threw us all off and pushed her way free to attack it again—just she and Hunk this time. They got the cap about a quarter off. Then they both dropped to their hands and knees, tugging at it. They dragged it away from the hole, over the gravel, with a terrible hollow iron sound. Finally they got it on its side, like an enormous wheel.

"Clear!" Cherry commanded. Hunk cleared. She dropped it with an enormous clang.

And there it was.

A hole.

We all gathered around. No one even spoke. A car passed on the highway, but none of us even looked up. God knows what the driver thought. All you could hear was Cherry's and Hunk's heavy breathing. The rest of us were almost holding our breath, as if we expected something or someone to crawl out of there. But there was nothing. Just a semi-dark hole with a metal ladder built right into the concrete wall, going down. You could see straight down for maybe ten feet, to a curved concrete floor. Then it turned, but you couldn't see where it went.

"Well," I said. But no one moved.

"Where's the water?" Krevitch asked.

"I think it's a storm tunnel," I said. "They're dry except during the rain."

"Do they lead to water?"

"They should. It's a combination system." I could smell just a hint of the old rotten-cabbage fumes.

Cherry peered down the hole. She cocked her

head sideways to listen. She even took off her aviation sunglasses.

"I don't hear anything," she said. She straightened up. "Just a minute!" She barreled over to the hearse herself this time, and returned in short order with a plastic bag and some rope.

She knelt down carefully by the hole. She opened the bag. She took out a dead, plucked fowl.

"Is that a chicken?" Hunk asked.

"A duck!" She grinned. She lashed a rope around its goose-pimpled neck. "They love these," she said. "In Florida, they sneak up under them in the water, when they're swimming. . . ." With one hand, she pantomimed a jaw. "Then they grab 'em by their webbed feet, and just drag 'em down!"

Krevitch shivered.

Cherry stood up. She moved into position over the hole, like someone ice-fishing.

"Hunk," she said, "have that crowbar ready, just in case."

"It's ready," Hunk answered, gripping it with both huge hands. The rest of us stood slightly behind him.

"If I say run, run!" Cherry said. "You never know what might come charging out!" She began to lower the duck into the hole slowly. She peered in after it, still lowering. It finally hit the floor with a plop. She waited a second. Then she jerked it a little, so that you could just make out the dull swishing sound of skin on the concrete. But nothing happened. When I looked down, all I saw was a dead duck lying on its side, smiling.

She jerked it up and down as though it were alive and hopping. Then she let it lie still again, waiting. . . .

"*Quack*," she tried, into the hole. "*Quack, quack*."

Nothing.

She looked at it. We all looked at it. We all looked at each other.

"I guess it's okay," she said. "Let's get the equipment."

We all walked over to the hearse to unpack the gear. There was tons of it—tarps and rolls and packs and sacks and a gigantic regulation Navy duffle bag, which Cherry commandeered immediately. There was even something that looked like a tent. And a camp stove. Aluminum paddles?

Cherry plopped down on the ground. She yanked off her combat boots and pulled on her hip boots.

"Cherry, do you really think we need all this crap?" I asked.

"You asked me that last time, too," she said struggling with her rawhide laces. "On the witch hunt! And who came up with the acetylene torch when you needed it?"

She had me there.

"Come on, you guys!" she ordered, still fighting the boots. "Get this gear out of the car and over to the hole." They all did as they were ordered. A few cars slowed as they came by, the drivers gawking.

"If anyone stops and asks," she said, "we're going camping in the city dump!" No one did stop, and no one asked. If anything, they speeded up, maybe worried for their lives.

Cherry jumped up with her sunglasses in her hand. Her eyes were blazing. "Wait!" she shouted. "Give me a minute!"

She began to stride—clumsily, in those hip boots—toward the hearse. She got inside. She started up the engine. For a second I thought she was abandoning us, but all she did was throw the thing into reverse and—to everyone's surprise—plowed backward at about forty miles an hour, off the road, across the ditch, and into the field. Milkweed went down, and ragweed, and Queen Anne's lace, and even a few small scrub sumacs, as the big yellow hearse disappeared into the field, backward. Grasshoppers flew up in clouds—and butterflies, and bees. Then the engine stopped, and the bent grass and weeds all sprang back up, and all we heard were birds again, and all we saw was field.

"Can you see it?" she called out from behind the weeds.

"No."

"Good." She appeared again, Jungle Jill, exhilarated. "Okay! Everybody pick up some of this crap and let's move!" She grabbed the big duffle bag herself. The rest of us took what we could. I gave Mary some smaller things, harpoons and a long

Army regulation flashlight, so that she could keep one hand free for her wildflowers. Krevitch staggered to the hole, completely submerged in camera equipment. Hunk looked like a walking baggage car. I carried the first-aid kit, the toolbox, and Mary's fifty-pound lunch bag.

We set everything down again at the opening.

"Okay, who's first?" Cherry asked.

Everyone looked at me.

Ten

I went down holding the toolbox in one hand.

It wasn't that hard. The rungs were sort of like those on the water tower we used to climb when we were kids. You just had to be careful, that's all. It got cooler, and there was that dead smell, but it was just cement. I could see the floor easily. The rungs of the ladder were rusty and filthy and cold. I could hear my own breathing. The faces above, peering down, seemed very small and distant and strange. But it was fine. I missed a rung and slipped and scraped my hand. I hit the floor with a slap. But it was fine.

"Okay," I said. *Okayyy* echoed in the icy air. It surprised me. I looked behind me. There was a tunnel. A large pipe, actually, leading off. . . .

"What's it like?" Cherry called down.

"It's fine," I said, with that terrible echo again. "It's all concrete. It reminds me of a burial vault."

Hunk came down next—with some prodding from Cherry. It was a bit of a squeeze, with his shovel and ropes and packs and all, but he got through the opening. The light cut out completely until he was halfway down the ladder. He missed the exact same rung I did, and fell with a crash.

"You okay, Hunk?"

He shook his head no, so he was fine.

Krevitch dropped some of his gear down first. Then he scampered down—surprisingly quickly, just like a little rat. His eyes were sparkling and his nose was twitching and I'd never seen him so alert. Hysterically alert. I reached up to help him on the tricky rung. I felt his whole body tremble. He screamed.

"It's just me, Krevitch!"

"I'm fine, I'm fine!" he said, giggling and shaking and jumping. He farted. Then he started to tremble again. I couldn't be sure in that light, but it looked as if he'd wet his pants, too.

Mary was next. I went halfway up the ladder to help her. She'd worn a dress again, so help me. Her pink panties looked flourescent as she descended. She came down very gracefully, one hand still holding the Queen Anne's lace.

"Don't drop your flowers," I said.

And she answered, very seriously, "I won't."

Cherry was last. We all cleared a space, a big space. She began dumping her gear down. First the duffle bag, then some grappling hooks—which just missed me. Then a mountain of rope, and what looked like a sleeping bag.

But no Cherry. She just stood up there.

"Come on," I called. "Onward and downward!"

But she didn't move.

"Come on," I said again.

"Okay, okay."

But she didn't come. She just continued to stare down at us. All we saw were those hip boots and the gigantic legs, clad in Army fatigues, the khaki jacket, the bayonet and . . .

A very scared face. A very doubtful face, gauging that hole. It took me a second to realize what it was. She didn't think she'd fit. Cherry was always very sensitive about her size.

"Don't worry," I called up gently. "Just ease yourself in, a little at a time."

"What if I get stuck?"

"We'll pull you."

"Not too hard," she said.

"No, no. Very gently."

So down came one foot, on the rung. Then the other. Then the first knee came into view. Then the second. Then the thigh—the space was filling up quickly. The other thigh. Total darkness suddenly. Krevitch flicked on the flashlight. Her bottom, that enormous bottom, had filled up the whole opening.

She stopped.

She was stuck.

She was shouting something, but we couldn't hear what.

"You grab one leg," I said to Hunk. "I'll take the other." We had to balance on that tiny ladder and pull—or pry, actually—first the left leg, then the right. The left again, then the right. Her fatigues scraped the cement side, and something ripped.

"Gently," I said. "Gently, *gently*." She was shouting again, maybe even screaming, but her voice was muffled above the fat. All we could do was continue easing her down, inch by inch. Her hips caught, solid. Mary had to climb up around us and push the flesh in hard, first one buttock and then the other. One of the hip boots came off in Hunk's hand. She seemed to be kicking too—or maybe just trying to signal us with her feet. We kept pulling. The key, it seemed, was the buttocks. Mary pressed and pushed, and Hunk and I pulled and *pulled*. Finally the body came free.

And down.

With a crash—and a scream. She landed on her enormous duffle bag, and on the lunch. Harpoons and supplies flew—sandwiches—pickles—everything. But she was down. A little scraped and ripped, but down.

"You okay, Cherry?"

She looked up at me with terrified eyes.

"Fine," she answered in a very husky voice. She stood up shakily and brushed off her seat, so gently and with such wounded pride that I suddenly felt a great rush of pity for old Cherry. I gave her a squeeze on the arm.

"Well done, Commander," I said, and smiled.

She smiled.

Then Mary smiled.

Krevitch smiled.

Hunk smiled.

We all smiled together.

Then we all started laughing, suddenly very satisfied with ourselves—laughing like crazy. Then we started clapping—and cheering—our voices echoing and hooting and making a terrific din. It was insane, but we'd made it! We were down there!

"Five-Star strikes again!" I shouted over the voices. Everyone laughed and cheered even louder. The echoes made it a mass of applause, like in an auditorium, so we all laughed and clapped and hooted and screamed even louder. It was one perfect moment when we were all united, our differences set aside and our fears and neuroses forgotten. Five-Star! All for one and one for all.

Friendship!

Alliance!

Success!

When the laughter had died down a little, Cherry finally said, "Hunk, you'd better pull that cover over, so no one comes by and sees an open manhole."

"Right," everyone said. "Do it."

So up the ladder he went. His big body filled the entire space for a second. Then you could see him straining and struggling with that gigantic grating. There was a series of enormous grunts as he held that iron cap just above his head, trying to lower it. It must have weighed a hundred pounds. The tension on his face was frightening, and for just a second, watching him straining and sweating, I suddenly had the most terrible feeling. It was like watching a man on the rack, or under some enormous torture. His eyes were rolling and he was gasping as the big cap came down slowly, slowly, like the top to a cage.

It fell into place with a terrible clang. He slid it around until it slipped into its exact mounting. That sound was even worse—a muffled crunch. And with it came the eeriest effect suddenly—bars of light across all of our faces, as if we were trapped in some kind of medieval dungeon.

I felt cold as death. I couldn't move. No one else moved, either. I don't think anyone else was even breathing. It was as if that same premonition had touched all of us. The silence was terrible after all that laughter.

Hunk came back down the ladder very hesitantly. He was feeling it too. We should have taken the hint right then, and climbed back up the ladder, and out. But we didn't. Instead we continued to study each other's faces, distorted by the bars of light. Even Mary looked monstrous, with only one eye lit and part of her mouth. . . .

Finally Cherry broke the spell. "That's the tunnel, huh?" she asked, her voice echoing.

Eleven

We walked a way in silence. We all kept bumping into one another because of the curved floor. It was just high enough for everyone to walk upright except me. I had to stoop.

"It's a pipe," Krevitch finally said.

"What did you expect—a roller rink?" Cherry asked, her voice filling the chamber.

Krevitch didn't answer. There were only echoes and silence, as we kept walking.

There seemed to be a very gradual curve to the pipe. You never could quite see to the end. There was always a rounded wall coming up. The cold seemed to be settling in more deeply, too, with each step, and the sulphur smell grew. It seemed to me that I could just make out some kind of engine sound in the distance, and the rush of water.

"What do we do if we run into a guard?" Krevitch asked.

"We tell them we're on a tour," Cherry answered immediately. "We started out at the plant, but we made a wrong turn." She said it with such conviction that you would have believed her, even knowing better.

"I don't think we'll run into anyone," Mary said. But then she stopped, stiff, staring, as if she really did see someone. I looked in the direction of the flashlight beam.

It was our first rat. It was just up ahead, sitting on the stone floor, its eyes right on us. It had red eyes, or eyes that shone red in the flashlight beam. It was large enough to run a cat easily. It didn't seem particularly surprised. It simply looked at us, with its whiskers flicking. The long leathery tail curled and uncurled slowly. Then the rat turned and began to move away down the tunnel at a fairly leisurely pace, almost hopping like a small kangaroo. It followed the curve into the darkness and disappeared.

"Was that a rat?" Mary asked.

"Yes," Krevitch answered.

"A big one," Hunk added.

We remained rooted to the spot.

"Come on," I finally said. "They don't like us any more than we like them." I tried to be casual, but something had run very cold in me, too, when I saw that animal. Just in the way it took us all in, one by one.

"Maybe it was a possum," Mary tried.

"Come on," I said.

Krevitch asked, "What if we run into a *pack*?"

"Take pictures!" Cherry said immediately. "It'll be great for the article!" I half-thought she was kidding until I looked at her face. She'd had just the opposite reaction to that animal. It thrilled her. She was absolutely glowing. "Have you got that infrared attachment?" she asked Krevitch. You'd better get it on, in case there's some real action!"

Krevitch took out his camera case and began to fumble. I could see that he was completely shot. His hand was shaking so badly that he couldn't even fit the pieces together.

"It's funny—" he said to his trembling fingers, which just couldn't control those parts, "—that there's nobody down here at all. Don't they guard this place?"

"What for?" I asked.

"In case someone breaks in."

"Who would?"

"We would!"

"Who else would be crazy enough?"

That stopped him. He couldn't think of anyone. He got the camera assembled. We all started walking again.

"Actually," Mary said, when we were all in step, "they did used to patrol down here once in a while. They found people living in here a couple times." Her voice echoed strangely.

"See?" Krevitch said, looking around as if he expected to run into a sewer gypsy at any moment.

"But now they only come down here for repairs," Mary continued. "And even then. . . ." She stopped, just as she had earlier. Only this time there was no rat.

"Even then—what?" I asked.

"They don't like to," she said. "My father usually has to come down here with them."

"Because of the alligators?" Krevitch asked, his eyes jumping.

"That," she said, "and . . ."

"And what?" I asked.

"Well, no one really knows for sure. . . ."

"Knows what?"

"Well . . . ." she said again. We were all looking at her now. Her pale hair glowed eerily in the dark, and even though she was trying very hard to be nonchalant, every word seemed more and more ominous. Even her breathy voice was chilly and strange.

"I'm not trying to scare anyone," she said.

"Just say what you were going to say."

"Well, a few years ago, one of the engineers . . ."

"Yes?"

"Disappeared."

"Disappeared?"

"Right down here somewhere. He never came back up."

"Completely disappeared?"

"To this day."

"They never found his body—or anything?"

"Nothing."

Hunk spoke, surprising everyone. "Maybe he just got tired of working in the sewer one day and took off," he said. "I always wanted to do that with my lawn-mowing."

We all continued to look at Mary. Our walking had slowed to baby steps again.

"Did they search the place?" I asked.

"As much as they could. There's hundreds of miles of these pipes, you know. And tanks and all. It would be almost impossible if he got underneath something, or inside. . . ."

"What do they think happened?"

"They don't know. Some people still think it's funny that nothing was ever found. If it had been animals, there would at least have been bones. . . ."

We all stopped again.

"Anyway," she said, "now if they do come down, they come in pairs. And armed. And they never do come down, except for emergencies. So we're safe."

She looked at all of our faces, but I don't think any of us felt too safe.

"I didn't mean to scare anyone," she began again. "Maybe I shouldn't have mentioned it."

There was silence for a second. Then Cherry said, "What a bit for the story! If we could only run across those bones!" No one answered. It was as if she were talking to herself. "Even just the skull!" she added. She began to look around, as if it might be in the storm tunnel.

"We gotta get to the water!" she suddenly added. "That's where the action is! Where's that map?"

I produced my photocopies. I held the flashlight so she could see. She had a hard time fitting the four sheets together.

"How the hell does this thing run?" she asked

the map. She had her nose about an inch from the print. She traced what she thought was the tunnel with one very dirty finger. "Look!" she said. "See?"

We all looked. It was impossible to see anything.

"*Conversion Tank*," she read. "That sounds like something where something comes together—or switches—doesn't it?" She looked up again, and around. When no one answered, she studied the map again, harder.

"It looks like it's right at the end of this tunnel. We don't know the actual distance, that's all. . . ." She looked up again and stared at the perpetual curve, as if trying to gauge how close we were, and to where. It seemed to be getting deadly cold now, and you could definitely hear water somewhere.

"Let's go," she said, inspired, it seemed, by the disappearing engineer. She even sniffed deeply, as if getting the scent. I had the flashlight, so I was dictating the pace. She pulled me on, faster. "What a scoop!"

You could hear water now clearly—the steady rush of water. And the dull, rhythmic sound of pumps. The smell was stronger too—so strong, suddenly, that we all began involuntarily to turn our faces sideways, as if to catch a fresh air current. But there were no air currents, fresh or otherwise. Just that flat, heavy, metallic stench. With each step it grew colder, the smell became more nauseating, and I found it harder to draw a breath.

Finally we had to stop.

"I think it's just around this bend!" Cherry said.

It was. We could hear it. The water flow was very near now, and we could feel the pumps in the cement under our feet. The smell couldn't have gotten any stronger.

Hunk had to say it. "It smells like shit."

"Bravo!" Cherry answered, but even that came out stifled. She was having trouble breathing herself. Krevitch was leaning up against the side of the pipe with his hand to his face, as though he were going to vomit. Mary had her eyes closed, and she was weaving. And I felt strangely lightheaded myself, almost drunk.

"Maybe we'd better wait a minute," I said. But Cherry was ready—always prepared. "I couldn't get the regulation gas masks," she said a little weakly, "but these are supposed to be good in a pinch. They use them in Tokyo whenever the smog gets heavy." She produced small squares of gauze with ties, like the masks surgeons use. She doled one out to each of us. They looked luminous in the dark. All I could think of was bandages.

"Come on," she said. "Put them on!"

We each put one on, without speaking. Once they were on, there was even less chance of speaking. Less chance of breathing, too, it seemed. But they did work, in a way, unless it was just the distraction.

We looked around at one another's eyes, like dizzy, trapped bandits.

"Let's go!" Cherry said, hoisting up her gear again. "Onward and inward!"

We turned the bend.

Twelve

It was like suddenly throwing open a door. The sound of water turned into a roar. The engines pounded like a powerhouse. The air became a thick, stinking mist, and even the light changed, it seemed—to green, or greenish.

"All right!" Cherry shouted loudly, right through the mask and over the pounding of the turbines. "This is more like it!"

It looked like an abandoned swimming pool, slimy with algae. The storm tunnel ran to the pool's edge. There was a ledge running around all sides, where you could step down. None of us did step down, though. We gathered at the rim of the tunnel, looking.

"Raw sewage," I tried to warn, but I could hardly hear my own words because of the pumps. The water—or whatever—was splashing thickly over the far edge of the pool, and running on through an even larger tunnel. There were pipes leading in from different areas, all splashing heavy gray waste into the choked pool. You could almost breathe the bacteria.

Cherry stepped down on the ledge. "Careful!" I said, but she didn't listen. She seemed transported. She studied the slime on the tiles, the floating sludge, the oily bubbles and the sticks and paper.

"Far out!" she said. "Krevitch! Get a couple shots of this from where you are! This is what we came for!"

Krevitch obeyed, teetering on the rim. I really thought he was going to topple in. But he got that camera positioned, and finally took a shot. Then another.

"Get that tunnel!" Cherry shouted over the motors. She pointed to the far edge of the pool, where a heavy cascade of sewage flowed over the edge and into a mammoth viaduct, like a subway tunnel, half above the water. The tunnel had small utility lights glowing in little cages on the walls, every twenty feet or so. They seemed to be flickering, unless it was just the rising gas distorting things. That dull, greenish haze hung over everything, as though the algae and ror were right in the air.

I stepped down on the ledge. Cherry was already halfway over to the other side of the pool. I helped Mary down. Then Krevitch. Even Hunk, who swayed strangely. Then we all made our way, single file, to a clearer section, a concrete landing on the far side of the pool. I kept trying to place the motors. Turbines, maybe, or some sort of heavy pumping equipment to keep this stuff flowing. It must have been behind the walls, though, or underneath us. You could hear it and you could feel it, but you couldn't see it.

When we got to Cherry, we all stood behind her and watched. She was leaning over the edge of the pool and looking in, as if she were contemplating a dive.

"Tom," she said, glancing up, "where's the duck?" She dropped her mask, grinning.

"Don't you think you ought to keep that on?" I asked, pointing to the limp gauze, hanging like a bib. "What about germs?"

She just laughed the most horrible laugh, so loud you could hear it over the engines. She looked so strange—so elated—that it suddenly struck me that maybe the methane gas was getting to her, making her high.

"Come on!" she said. "I need that duck! Krevitch, get the camera ready!"

I couldn't find the duck at first. It was in with one of the bags or bundles somewhere. Finally I found it next to the cooking stove. Even the bird looked odd now. Absurd. Even the rope, the plastic bag—everything. Hunk pulled off his soggy gauze mask and *he* looked strange. It was as if we were all from another world, ridiculously out of place.

Cherry searched through her duffle bag and pulled out three harpoons. She passed them around.

"Only if it's a big one," she said. "If it comes over the ledge or anything—then go for the belly. But if it's a small one . . ." She started digging around in her bag again. She pulled out a huge, heavy net. ". . . then use this. I want to bring it back alive. We can always donate it to the zoo."

She stood there and looked at us all for a moment, like a sergeant inspecting the troops.

"Ready?" she asked, swinging the duck.

We all nodded.

She turned around to the pool and threw in the bird. It landed on top of the thick sewage with a plop, and then lay there on its side, with its bill in the muck.

"This is is worse than dog days on Lake Winnebago," Cherry said. She yanked the rope a few times. The duck slid over the slime like a hockey puck over ice, but it still wouldn't go down. She yanked it again, cursing, and this time it found a gap in the growth. It slipped slowly into the water. It went down even more slowly, as though it were sinking in oil.

Only an inch or two of the rope moved at a time. Then more. Then more.

"It's going down," she said, letting out the line.

She tensed, waiting for the big strike. The rope kept playing out. It was deeper than you'd think, maybe ten feet or so.

She pulled the rope slightly, as if she might have a nibble. Nothing.

Hunk got a better grip on his harpoon and positioned himself, like a palace guard. Mary was still gripping those poor wildflowers in one hand. She held her harpoon in the other.

"We've got the advantage when it comes up," Cherry said. "We've got the height."

"I think it's too cold in here for alligators," I said. It had to be about fifty degrees.

"It's warmer down there," she answered. "See the steam?" And she stood hunched over that pool like The Old Fisherman. She had enormous concentration when she needed it.

"That's gas, not steam," I said. "Besides, I don't think anything could live in this."

But she just played out her rope. She even walked down the side a little, trolling. She was trying so hard that, demented or not, you had to hope for her.

Suddenly she stopped.

She stiffened up. The rope was straight.

"You got a bite?" I asked.

"Feels like it." She braced herself, motioning us all around with her head.

"Be careful," Mary said, suddenly very protective. She got up close to Cherry, as if to lend a hand if needed.

"Krevitch," Cherry said tensely, "get the camera ready."

It was ready.

I put one of my hands on the rope for a feel. "Maybe it's just snagged," I said.

"Start to pull in," she answered. "Slowly." She was whispering, as if it might sense us through the rope.

The drag was terrific. We pulled in a foot of slime-coated rope. Then there was a heavy tug, and it stopped. No matter how hard we pulled, it wouldn't give.

"Careful now," she said, "or we'll snap it. Hunk!"

Hunk joined us, his huge hands gripping the rope just above mine.

"Gently," Cherry said. "*Gently*." Hunk was amazingly gentle, like an obedient machine.

The line began to give again, but with definite resistance.

"We've got him," Cherry said. "Get the harpoons ready. Get the net ready. Get the camera ready. Get ready!" Krevitch held the camera, and Hunk and Cherry and I were on the rope. Mary held the net, three harpoons, and her flowers.

"Okay," Cherry said, talking to the rope, which came in inch by green inch. "Come to mama."

There *was* something alive on that line. There was the strangest give and take. Just when we thought it was snagged, there was a give. Now we could feel a dead weight, as we pulled it off the bottom. We were pulling something up.

"Get ready," she said for the tenth time.

"Get ready," she added.

Then she asked, pulling steadily, "You guys ready?"

Suddenly the foam and sludge and algae and scum at the very top of the pool parted. The edge of something round and black broke the surface slowly, heavily. Then it rolled back down again, just beneath the sludge. You couldn't quite tell. . . .

"It looked like a tire," I said. I almost laughed. Just like the old joke.

"Bullshit," Cherry said. She yanked angrily at the line. The thing broke the surface again, round and black and rubbery.

"Aw," Hunk said, disappointed.

It did look like a tire. A tractor tire maybe. But Cherry wouldn't be satisfied until she saw the *Goodyear* on the side. She pulled even harder. It broke the surface again and lay on the scum. It was harder than ever to see when you had to. I let the line go slack. Cherry did too. The tire didn't sink back down, though. It just lay there.

Looking at us.

It had a head, with a red slash on each side of its cheeks.

And eyes.

The head rose right up, on a long skinny neck, out of the black. The head had a long pointed snout, with two enormous eyes. The mouth opened, showing a thick pink tongue. It hissed. Algae fell from the beak—or jaws—whatever it was that hung open, hissing. The rope was tangled around the head and neck, and underneath the round black body.

It began to paddle with two huge front paws. Four paws, pushing at the scum. The paws had nails, like talons. The thing crawled or swam right over the slime—rope and all—to the edge of the pool. Its two front paws came up one at a time, right onto the ledge by our feet. We could hear the bony claws scrape cement. The stench was unbelievable. The back legs came up now, trying to hook onto the ledge for a foothold. They caught, and the thing lunged up, dripping algae and sewage.

Thirteen

Cherry screamed.

Mary screamed.

Krevitch screamed.

Hunk and I were stupefied. I'd never seen anything like it in my life. Yes I had. But not that big. It was a gargantuan, slimy, mud-covered turtle.

"It's a turtle!" I shouted through the noise. "It's just a turtle! Relax!" Everyone stopped screaming and started gaping. Even the old turtle seemed to hang in suspension for a moment, with a duck leg sticking out of its mouth. Then it made one final lunge with those back legs—eyes bulging, neck straining, and nostrils snorting green bubbles.

"Krevitch—get a shot of that!"

He did. I had to give him credit. He got himself together long enough to step forward and immortalize the beast; hanging almost in midair between the tank and the landing. Then the turtle did a spectacular flip backward and landed belly-shell up, with a huge splash, in the pool. It slowly submerged, sideways, leaving only oily yellow bubbles and bits of duck meat.

Cherry pulled the rope in, just as slowly. There was only a small bit of the duck's head left, attached. For all her fervor, she seemed a little shaken.

"I didn't know turtles ever got that big," she said.

"It looked just like my dimestore turtle," Hunk said. "Juniper." Everyone stared at him. "Only bigger," he added.

"That probably *was* somebody's dimestore turtle," I said.

Krevitch, covered with sprayed sludge from the turtle's plunge, shivered as he said, "Well, we got the pictures anyway."

"That's enough," Mary added, shivering a little herself. Her hair was coated with strings of algae and slime, and her legs were all strangely mottled from the cold. She sneezed, and her mask flew down. She let it hang.

"I can't stand this stink anymore," Hunk complained. His mask was still up, but it was nothing but a mass of saliva. He pulled it off. He looked even worse.

"That's a good enough story, isn't it, Cherry?" I asked. She was over on the ledge, rolling up the rope over her shoulder, just like a seaman. She didn't seem to hear. She just kept staring at that ripped-off duckhead.

"What?" she asked.

"That's our story—okay? Everyone's cold, and the smell's getting to be too much. Let's go back."

"Are you serious?" she asked, turning around.

"Everyone's sick," I repeated.

She looked around at us all, wet and covered with sewer spray, as if we were insane. "That's our story?"

"Why not?"

"*Turtle Discovered in Cuty Sewer*"?

"Giant turtle. . . ."

"You think people don't know that?" she asked, shouting. "You think that's going to surprise them? They'll laugh us off the campus!" She had a terrible look on her face, as if she could actually picture herself being hooted down Library Lane.

"I've got to be home by three," Mary said.

"We've only been down here a few minutes," Cherry answered.

"Two hours," Krevitch corrected.

"Two hours?" I asked. It seemed impossible. I checked my watch. It was true.

"We came down here to find alligators!" Cherry said. "And I'm not going back with pictures of a turtle! You think a *turtle* ate that engineer?"

It seemed possible. . . .

Finally I said, as diplomatically as possible, "We'd better vote, like always."

Cherry glared at me and then at her duckhead.

"All right," she said. "Who wants to go back with a picture of a goddam turtle and get laughed off the campus—and who wants to go on and finish what we came for?"

Hunk raised his hand.

No one else knew what we were voting for.

"That settles it," Cherry said. "We stay." She began to coil her rope again.

"Wait a minute," I said. "Run this by us again. Who wants to leave?"

Mary raised her hand. Krevitch raised his. I raised mine.

Hunk looked at all of us, and finally raised his.

"Hunk—you asshole!" Cherry said. "You can't vote both ways!"

"Hunk," I said gently, "what do you want to do? Go? Or stay?"

"Okay," Hunk answered.

"That's one for me," Cherry said quickly. "Three against two. We always go four-out-of-five, remember?"

"Hunk," I repeated, "do you want to go, or do you want to stay?"

Hunk sneezed horribly. He wiped his nose on his jacket sleeve. "When are we getting out of here?" he asked, as if I hadn't even spoken. "I'm getting the flu."

"We'd better go," I said to Cherry.

She hesitated for a second.

Then—amazingly—she said, "Okay."

Just like that. No scene or anything. And she bent over to gather her things—the harpoons, the rope, the duckhead. Slowly she stuffed it all back into her regulation duffle bag. She was so agreeable that we all looked at each other uneasily.

Then she came around to each of us. She took our supplies right out of our hands—all the little bags and bundles, the toolbox, the first-aid kit, everything but the lunch. She stacked it all on the ground, like baggage at a train station.

"Okay, you guys," she said in a very small, hurt voice. "I'll see you later."

"What?"

"I'll see you all later," she repeated.

"You're not coming with us?"

"No." Her voice was almost tearful, and she wouldn't look any of us in the eye. "I'll see you all later."

"You're going to stay here?"

She wouldn't look up. She took the net in her hands, all neatly folded, like a flag. "I know they're down there," she said. "It's just something I've got to do. You guys go back. I'll catch up with you later."

"You've got the keys to the hearse," Krevitch said.

She never broke character. She dug down into one of the sacky pockets of her fatigues and pulled the keys out, along with some fishing line and bubble gum. She handed the keys over to me.

"You can drive the car back," she said. "I'll catch up with you all later."

"How will you get back?"

"Hitchhike."

"With all this equipment?"

"I'll manage."

"I've got the camera," Krevitch reminded her.

She looked as if she hadn't thought of that. She fingered the net awhile. "Then I'll just have to bring it back alive," she said.

I could see her out on the highway, thumbing her way home with a live alligator in a net.

"Come *on*, Cherry."

But she wouldn't budge. "I'll manage," she repeated. "You guys go on. Don't worry, I'll give you all credit in the article."

"We voted that we'd all go."

"So go," she said. "All of you . . ." And she looked forlorn, like an outcast, which is exactly how she'd always pictured herself, I suppose.

Then she started her monologue all over again. This is the first chance we've ever had to make a real smash. This beats the Pigeon Lady, the witches, the bakery. This even beats that picture of the mayor. I'm not going to throw away the chance of a lifetime."

She burned her eyes into the fetid steam over the pool, as though she were having a vision. "There's something down there," she said. "I can feel it."

"We voted," I repeated.

"I know just where they are, too." She turned her eyes toward the far side of the pool, near the tunnel exits. "They're on the bottom, over there. They like the warm, dark places. Warm, dark places . . ."

She began to walk slowly in that direction, as if she were in a trance.

"We can't leave you here, Cherry," I said.

"Five more minutes and you guys would have been in on the scoop of the year," she said, her back to us, walking away into the murk. She had.

the same discouraged slouch to her huge old
shoulders that she'd had the first time she'd ever
walked into the Journalism Office, to join Five-
Star. That was when she'd come in twentieth in a
field of twenty for Homecoming Queen. Some
fraternity had run her as a joke, and she'd taken it
all very seriously. She'd even dieted. Then those
returns had come in, and the laughter had started . . .

"They told Magellan to turn back, too," we
heard her say in the distance.

We all looked at one another. Even Krevitch
seemed to sympathize a little with those hang-dog
shoulders and the broken voice. It was like seeing
an old champ go down in the ring.

"Maybe we could stay five more minutes," he
said. "What if she gets lost or something? You
know what happened to that engineer."

You could barely see her now. Just a hulk, with
packs on her back and gear in both hands, like
Bigfoot disappearing into the swamp.

"Five more minutes then," I said, sighing.

Mary sighed, too. "I know this is a mistake," she
said.

"Cherry!" I called loudly. "Wait!"

Fourteen

An hour later, she finally had the net underneath the water, on the far side of the tunnel. It had a rope attached to each corner. Hunk held one rope, I held one rope, Krevitch held one rope, and Mary held one rope.

"When I say pull," Cherry said, "pull!" She had one of Mary's classic sandwiches in her hand. Polish sausage and alfalfa sprouts, with mustard. She took a good bite, chewed, and studied the sluggish flow of water. She got down on her hands and knees—still chewing—and peered into the murk.

"There it is," she whispered.

We all looked, holding our ropes. The water over here was more water, less sludge. You could see down a short distance. There *was* something moving around down there, slowly.

"See it?" she whispered.

We all saw it, whatever. It was long and serpentine, and moving lazily, so slowly that it appeared to be crawling along the bottom. It was just to the right of the submerged net. It seemed to turn shades, from lighter to darker.

"That's the belly," Cherry said, "when it turns sideways. It's about four feet long."

"Maybe we ought to try for a smaller one," I suggested.

"The bigger, the better," she answered. I could see the picture of Five-Star, flanking an enormous alligator: *What's in Your Sewer?*

"Why is it rolling around?" Krevitch asked.

"Exercise, probably," she answered. "Now listen! When you get it up, remember—flip the net over! Don't give it a chance to slash its way out! Tangle it up! I don't want to have to use this." She brandished her harpoon. "Also," she said, "remember—the power is all in the top jaw. So if it starts snapping, clamp down the top jaw."

"Isn't it the bottom jaw?" I asked. "The one with the hinge?"

Cherry blanked. She clomped on her own jaws a couple of times, as if checking. "One of them, anyway," she said. "Whichever one is moving— grab it and hold on! They can close, but they can't open!"

She hovered over the spot again. "Okay," she said, dangling a piece of Polish sausage, "ready?"

"Ready."

She plopped it into the water. It went straight down, leaving a little string of mustard and a few grease bubbles on the surface.

The swimming/crawling thing moved right over the net area to investigate.

"*Pull!*" Cherry shouted, her harpoon raised.

We pulled. We had something. Mary's end was

a little weak, and Hunk yanked his up too quickly, but we had it. You could feel enormous plunges of something alive in the net—shooting first to one side, then the other. Heavy—angry—so much fury side to side that Mary was having a hard time controlling her end.

"Easy now—easy!" Cherry cried.

Hunk was hauling in like a madman. His end came up first. There was a furious slapping—big waves of foamy, filthy water. All we could see was suds and the thing—whatever—plunging from one side of the net to the other, as the water became shallower and shallower.

"Now—together!" Cherry directed, when we had the net about a foot from the surface. We all gave a final heave, and the big bundle of twisting, turning net splashed up out of the water. Filth covered us—I got a patty of algae in the eye—but we dragged it up over the ledge and onto dry land. You still couldn't really see what it was—just that jerking, jumping bundle of net with the rolling thing inside, tangled and trapped.

"Okay now—stand back!" Cherry shouted, her harpoon still raised. I grabbed for my harpoon, too. Hunk, too. Krevitch grabbed his camera, and Mary even dropped her flowers as she snatched up a wrench.

It jumped. Whatever it was—it jumped. The net jumped with it, a tangled mass, about a foot into the air. It landed with an enormous clap. Then the whole thing twisted and turned convulsively.

"Pin down the net with your spears!" Cherry screamed. We all did, stabbing at the edges of the net, leaning down on our harpoons, pressing until the handles bent. Part of the net opened anyway, and an enormous tail flipped out and beat the concrete, slapping up and down. Huge scales flew everwhere—and slime, and water.

"It's a fish!" I shouted.

"A fish?" Cherry looked outraged.

"A fish," Hunk repeated.

"A goldfish," said Krevitch. "But look at the size!"

It was huge, maybe half as big as Krevitch himself. At least fifty pounds.

I opened the net a little. It just lay on the concrete, big-eyed and gulping. It had enormous, dull, plastic-like scales and a thick head. It was the fattest fish I'd ever seen.

"It's a carp," I said. " A grown-up goldfish."

"A goldfish," Hunk echoed, probably remembering his own.

"Oh," Mary said, "poor thing. Throw it back— quick."

"Get a picture, Krevitch," Cherry said, but without any real enthusiasm. The dull lighting from the small utility lights reflected off the scales as the fish heaved and gulped, making it look very rare and exotic in all that filth. I couldn't help but have the same feeling I'd had earlier with the duck: it seemed so unnatural to see something natural down here.

"Throw it back in," Mary repeated.

"Throw it back my ass!" Cherry answered, pulling out her hunting knife. "We need it for bait!"

I blocked Cherry's way. "Bait for what?"

"For the 'gators!"

"No," I said. "That's it. We're over our time limit. We're going back."

"We're going back? With pictures of a dimestore turtle and a goldfish? That's what we're going back with?"

"That's what we're going back with."

"From 'Good Night, Irene' to a goldfish?"

"Sorry. . . ."

She looked around from face to face. She didn't get much support. Everyone else looked nauseated.

"I'm sorry," Mary said. "But I told you—"

"*You've got to be home by three!*" Cherry mimicked. "I know, I know!"

"I don't feel too well, either," Mary added.

No one did. Even Cherry looked a little green now.

"Come on you guys, help me," I said. I hoisted my end of the net up. They all hoisted theirs, too.

"One, two . . . on three!"

We flipped the net over the ledge, and the jumbo goldfish plunged out and over. It hit the thick water hard, on its side. Scales flew like fireworks. Its tail caught a few lumps of something sloppy and splashed it up into our faces, in farewell. A fine, putrid spray showered down on all of us, making the smell that much more pungent— like a fertilized lawn, after a light rain.

"Let's go," I called, wiping waste from my cheek.

"Okay," Cherry answered—resigned, it seemed. "Anyway," she said, wringing out a section of her net, "we got a couple good pictures. I suppose it's a story just coming down here."

"That's right," I said, amazed. I suppose I should have been more suspicious, knowing Cherry. But I've always been a believer. She seemed ready to go—glazed in the eyes, like all of us.

"Krevitch," she said, "before we go, get a shot of me folding up the net."

Krevitch did.

"Now get one of all of us, loaded down with gear!"

So we all lined up, and Krevitch shot us, with the culvert oozing in the background.

Cherry looked around. "Let's make sure we didn't miss anything. We won't be coming back! How about Hunk and Tom, peering down into all that crap?" So Hunk and I crawled to the edge of the tank and peered into the water.

"Fish around with your harpoons," she said, "like you're prodding something."

I prodded a drain. I came up with a spearful of green toilet paper.

"That's good," she said.

I got up unsteadily. "Okay, let's go."

"All right," Cherry answered. But then she said, "Hey—"

"No more, Cherry. That's enough. Come on."
That last one had gotten to me.

"Just a quickie!" she said. And then, very un-
usually for her, "Please! Look! Wouldn't that be a
perfect shot? That thing over there . . . ?"

Fifteen

It was sort of intriguing. . . .

It was a little train, right inside the huge tunnel, leading out. It was perched on top of the ledge, and loaded down with pipe sections. It looked like one of those kiddie rides at the zoo, three or four cars with the little engine in the back. It must have been used for pipe repairs, or inner-sewer hauling. It ran right alongside a catwalk, for as far as you could see.

"We've got to get a picture of that!" Cherry said. "With us on top the pipes! And all our gear! Classic? '*Sewer Safari*'! No! '*Sewer Tour*'! Hahaha! Krevitch, can't you put that thing on timer and crawl up with us?"

"I guess," Krevitch answered.

"Like we're taking off for the Interior!" Cherry continued, leading us all over there. "Perfect!" She laughed that horrible laugh of hers again, and this time it echoed through the new section, the tunnel.

"Just one now," I said—the same thing I'd been saying for hours. She didn't even answer. She was making her way very gingerly over the little cat-walk that spanned the tunnel.

"We should go back," Mary said. "Right now. I just have the feeling . . ."

I did too, but I followed that little procession right over the catwalk, just the same.

"Make a wish!" Cherry said, throwing a penny into the muck. I made the same wish I'd always made—peace with Mr. Malgren—and gave Mary a little squeeze.

But the penny just floated on the surface.

"It's amazing," Krevitch began again, "that there's no one down here at *all*. This equipment must be worth a fortune!"

"It reminds me of the Lionel train I got for my birthday," Hunk said.

"When you were little?" Mary asked, without thinking.

"Last month," he answered.

"Okay!" Cherry began, directing operations. "Hunk, you're the biggest"—not technically true—"so you get in the first car. 'Cause we're shooting from the back. See? By the engine. Get it?"

Whether he did or not, Hunk crawled up into the far car.

"Tom, you and Mary in the middle. We like to keep our little Friends together—hahaha!" She was in surprisingly good spirits again. Mary and I crawled up over some banded concrete tubes and found a comfortable spot.

"And I'll get in front," Cherry said—which

was the back, by the engine. "Krevitch, after you set up the timer, you hop in here with me."

"Okay," Krevitch agreed. He had a small tripod set up about ten feet away, on the concrete ledge. Then he used his light meter. Then a couple more dials and settings. Krevitch always tried to do things very professionally. He was a miserable photographer, actually—third-string relief on the *Varsity Press* sports page—but he always made the effort.

"Everybody get where you're going to be," Krevitch called.

We were.

"And look happy!" Cherry ordered. "Like you've just climbed Everest!"

So we looked happy. Sick to our stomachs, but happy.

"Okay," Krevitch said. He walked out from behind the camera. "We've got twenty seconds." He ran over to the train. Cherry reached down and with one mighty heave yanked him up into the front car—actually the back car—with her.

"When?" Cherry asked.

"It'll buzz," Krevitch answered. "About twelve seconds now."

We remained perfectly still, with our smiles frozen.

"Maybe the lights for this thing should be on," Cherry said, looking down at all the levers and switches. I knew that was a mistake. She threw one. The lights did come on—a big headbeam, and a tailbeam, and little red lights, all along the side. But something else came on, too—a terrific rush of power, like on an electric streetcar.

"Now we've got it!" Cherry laughed, and positioned herself behind the controls. "Let's make it look like I'm driving. Smile, everyone!"

"Cheese," Hunk said.

I smiled. Mary smiled.

There was the terrible feeling of gears meshing. "Cherry—" I shouted.

"It's buzzing!" Krevitch said. "Smile!"

"All aboard!" Cherry called.

The train started to move. The camera flashed. Mary screamed something, and Krevitch lost his balance and almost fell out. Even Cherry looked confused. No one knew what was happening. The camera started moving farther and farther away. Cherry fumbled with the same lever, but it wouldn't budge. There were three or four small handles in a row, like switches on a power box. She tried the next one. We picked up speed.

"My camera!" Krevitch shouted, trying to crawl out of the train. "My camera!"

Cherry looked horrified, fighting with the second lever. I crawled out of my car, over to hers. We were deep inside the tunnel now, doing maybe twenty miles an hour. The utility lights on the walls were flying by faster and faster.

"Maybe this one," I shouted. It must have been third gear. The thing really began to roll. Mary was shouting my name over and over from the other car, the damp air was whistling, and the echoing noise from the pipes and wheels on the rails was incredible. When I looked back at Mary, she was shouting at Hunk, "Duck! Duck!" All I could think of was the bird. Then I realized—a long, low ceiling coming up. A new part of the tunnel system, very narrow and tight. Hunk ducked, just missing the concrete overhang. Mary ducked. Cherry and I ducked. Krevitch didn't have to duck. One of the metal harpoons was sticking up, though, and hit the stone and went flying, with sparks and clatter. It spun off into the water. We were doing forty now, at least, with no one saying a word. We were all just hanging on. The little open cars were swaying crazily and jumping at each rail joint. The pipe sections were rolling too, and we had to shift and dodge to keep from being crushed.

"It's jammed!" Cherry screamed. "It won't stop!"

We took a turn. Everyone held tight, but the centrifugal force was too much. We all flew right, and the cars lurched way to one side. Some supplies flew out—the canvas packsack, the toolbox, tarps and bundles—all bouncing wildly on the tracks behind us. There had to be a brake. Everything that moves has a brake. I kept searching for a handle or lever or paddle or bar.

"Is this electric?" I yelled over the noise.

"I don't know!" Cherry yelled back.

There had to be a wire to cut, or plug to pull. I pulled at some wires. I pulled at a knob. I yanked out what looked like a spark plug. But the thing kept going. In fact, it went faster. We crossed a kind of intersection and veered off in a new direction. We seemed to be going up, and then we seemed to be going down. It was impossible to gauge. Sometimes the thing seemed to be losing power on a climb, like a roller coaster, but then it would pick up again.

"Maybe we should jump if it slows down again!" I shouted. But Mary was frozen, and Hunk and Krevitch too. We were out of the pipes entirely now, it seemed—like in some kind of subway. There were piles and piles of concrete sections and iron tubes and cinderblocks and reinforcement rods everywhere, as though something was under construction, or repair.

"This might be the end of the tracks," Cherry said.

But it wasn't the end of anything. We rolled right by all the building materials and veered off into a different section. We chugged up a little incline. The speed slowed, with the effort, and I thought about jumping again. I stood up to see. There was a terrific series of spurts and sparks—buzzing and pops and blue flashing just above my head—and only then did I realize where the power was. It was in two lines that ran above the tracks. There was a long arm running from the side of my car to the wires. All I had to do was force the end free from the wires. I took the harpoon and wrapped the net around the handle. I pushed at the bar, on the rubber-coated base. Then higher and higher, until the arm flew free from the wires. There was a terrific spray of blue sparks, and a jumping and catching and jumping again, as the contact point hit the wire and left the wire and hit the wire again, with each lurch of the car. The engine cut on and off, and the lights too—and with it, the gears, so that it was all a series of lurches and jerks and jumps, knocking everyone and everything up and down, back and forth. But when I gave it a final push and held it, everything died—the engine, noise, lights—everything.

"You did it!" Cherry shouted.

But I hadn't. We were still rolling, fast as ever. The only difference was the noise. There was no engine now, just a steady coasting down a decline—powerless, silent, but clicking down the rails as steadily as ever.

"It'll stop," I shouted, even though now I didn't really have to shout. "It has to! As soon as we level off. It'll come right to a standstill. Just hang on. It has to stop."

Sixteen

It didn't.

We coasted on. Soon we were gliding downhill faster than ever. At first I thought it was simply momentum.

"As soon as it levels off . . . ," I repeated. Everyone looked at me, but no one said a word. We were all crouching and waiting. It was bizarre to hear the wheels on the rails and to see the small, dim lights flickering by, even after the engine had stopped—as if some outside force were pulling us along on its own.

The area was wider now and lighter. Then narrower and darker. Warmer and then colder again. We whizzed down and on.

The tracks split in various directions. We never knew which one the train would follow. It just followed. Sometimes it seemed that we were out of the tunnels completely—on top of the tunnels, or beside the tunnels. Maybe they changed shapes or functions. Sometimes there was water below, and sometimes the water was more at the side. Sometimes we were a few inches out of the water, and sometimes we were over a cement landing, like the island at a bus stop. Each time we took a turn, the thing would slow and I'd think we were finally going to coast to a stop. But it never did stop.

"It's slowing," I said finally. It seemed to be. The little lamps on the walls weren't spinning by with such insane speed now. It was warmer, and the air was better. I still had to shout some over the noise of the wheels on the tracks, but everyone seemed a little more composed. "The minute it stops we'll just climb out and find an exit," I said. "Don't worry—they're all along here."

We scattered a pack of rats up ahead in the distance, milling around the tracks. They spread out like a large ink stain to every side of the the tunnel, disappearing into holes in the cement, some just above the water. They didn't even let us get up close this time. It was strange, but they seemed shyer in packs. No one even mentioned them.

We were slowing. I could feel it now.

That's when I saw the figure. I didn't know if anyone else did or not. Maybe they were all still spellbound by the tracks or the rats. It looked like a little old man, with long white hair, way up ahead—above us—on a catwalk. He was dressed in a ragged outfit, and clutching what looked like a heavy black length of sewer pipe. Despite his appearance, I thought he might be some kind of sewer worker or maintenance man. Maybe they dressed that way down here—or hired hippies.

I almost called out—almost waved. But the fig-

ure started to move to one side of the catwalk, and
there was something so wild and jerky in the
movements that I checked myself. Immediately after that we turned. There was a tremendous clang
of something—iron—hitting the tracks, sending re-
verberations you could feel right through the
wheels and car, up your spine.

Then I realized what it was.

There was a small mountain of iron pipes
ahead, piled on the tracks.

Hunk hollered first. Then Mary. Then Krevitch. Everyone started waving and screaming, but
we couldn't stop. There was nothing to do but
crouch down in the car and wait. I grabbed
Cherry and pulled her to the floor.

We hit the pipes with an enormous crash. You
could feel the cars jumping off the track—and a
horrible wrenching, as each tipped the next sideways. I saw the front car fly off the track and
topple left, toward the water. The second car—
Mary's—flipped up, but stayed halfway on the
track. My car rammed the second car, and that's
all I really saw or could remember seeing. I flew,
along with Cherry's duffle bag, and landed somewhere and rolled on something and hit something,
and all I could see after that—vividly, but with a
kind of dull nausea—was Mr. Malgren sitting on
his living room sofa with a can of beer in his hand.
He was smiling very amiably and telling me how
happy he was that I was dating Mary, and that he
looked forward to my being his son-in-law and to

all the nice Sunday chicken dinners we'd have together. . . .

*

I was kneeling down, holding my head.

"Here," Mary was saying. "Use this." It was a
piece of her dress. It was all blood.

"Are you okay?" I asked. It didn't sound like my
voice.

"Fine," she answered. "Don't talk now. She
pressed the rag harder to my head. When I managed to focus my eyes and look up at her, she
didn't look fine at all. Her face was filthy, and
there was a reddish bruise on her temple.

"Just sit still a second," she said. Cherry was
there too, standing over me. She looked pretty
filthy too, but not hurt. Krevitch was there, shaking.

"Is he okay?" Cherry asked Mary, as if I
couldn't hear.

"I think so," Mary answered. She too talked as
though I weren't there. And maybe I wasn't. Suddenly I was having another vision. Mr. Malgren
was making all the wedding arrangements, asking
if we'd prefer a trip to Barbados for our honey-
moon, or maybe something for the apart-
ment. . . .

I heard Krevitch say, "Hunk's out cold. I think
he's hurt bad."

That did it. I got up. My head was throbbing,
and even my teeth, but I got up. I took a look at

the wreckage. I couldn't believe those cars—couldn't believe that we'd all even gotten out of there in one piece. One—the first—was dangling right over the edge, down into the water. One had been rammed straight up; it was standing on two hind wheels. One—mine—was on its side. There were pipes and jagged pieces of pipes all over, but you could still see the remainder of the original mound on the tracks.

Hunk was lying by the tracks, soaking wet and covered with filth.

"I had to haul him out of the water," Krevitch said. I couldn't imagine that, but Krevitch was soaked up to his groin. Hunk was bleeding from his nose and mouth, and dead-still. His head was propped on top of his soaked jacket. He was greenish-white, and he really did look hurt.

"Hunk?"

No answer. I tried feeling for a pulse on the bottom of that wrist. I don't know if I felt one or not. The vein was cold and wet and hard, and I just couldn't be sure.

His ears were bleeding.

His eyes opened—those big, bloodshot, mongoloid eyes.

"Hunk," I said again.

His eyes only blinked. They didn't really even look. It was strange. Somehow they weren't Hunk's eyes at all. The last bit of expression seemed to have gone out of them.

The eyes rolled around and took us all in. But

his head didn't move, and he still didn't say anything.

"Hunk, are you all right?"

"Sure," he answered. Just that one word. It wasn't his voice, and I couldn't ever remember Hunk using that word before, at least not like that.

He didn't say anything else. He didn't try to get up, either.

"Hunk, does anything hurt?" I asked. I touched his legs a little, and his arms.

"Nope," he answered in that same foreign voice, without looking at any of us.

"Just lie there a minute," I said—not that he could do anything else. He stared up at the ceiling.

"Maybe it's shock," Cherry suggested. All scratched and battered, she looked as if she were in shock herself. Mary too, and Krevitch. Everyone looked blank and helpless.

Hunk started vomiting. I moved his head sideways, to let it flow to the ground. I wiped his face and mouth clean with my hand. He vomited again and again, small amounts of mucus and sour sandwich, and finally nothing—just the wretching and gagging, with nothing coming up.

Then he lay back again, looking.

"We'll wait awhile," I said. "Then we'll have to get some help." Which wasn't really saying anything at all. Just words. Everyone looked at me, and at Hunk, and at our surroundings—the tunnels and chambers and lights. But I didn't have anything more to say, and no one else did, either. Not even Cherry.

For the first time since we'd been together, I think, none of us really had any idea what to do.

Seventeen

Cherry swabbed everyone with hydrogen peroxide and passed around a few bandages. She used two entire rolls of gauze on Hunk's head. There wasn't much we could do after that, so we all rested awhile, using the concrete pipe sections for chairs and head props.

We tried to think.

"Did any of you," I asked, after a few minutes of rest, "see anything back there—when we were coming around the track? Just before we hit the pipes?"

"Like what?" Cherry asked from her cement cot. She looked uncomfortable lying there, but too exhausted to adjust her bulk.

"A person?" I said. "Up high, on the catwalk. Holding a pipe section."

"No," she answered, after a pause. She had a hell of a look on her face. "Did you?"

"I'm not sure," I replied—to take away that look, and Mary's, too. There was no need to terrify them all, and besides, I wasn't absolutely sure myself. Not after that blow to the head. It might have been a shock trip, like the visions of Mr. Malgren.

"I didn't see anyone," Krevitch said.

"I didn't either," Mary added, but you could see when she looked at me that she knew I had.

"Someone had to pile up those pipes like that," I tried.

Cherry answered, after a nervous pause, "Sometimes kids get down in places like this and do those kinds of things."

"I don't think kids could get down here," I said.

"Workmen, then," Mary said. "Maybe they were building something."

"And left them on the track?"

"Maybe this whole area is closed down," she suggested. "That train didn't look like it was in use." She must have felt the weakness in her own words, though, because she didn't continue.

I let it go. I didn't want to believe anything else, either.

But then Hunk spoke, without moving, without even blinking. "I saw someone," he said in that same peculiar voice.

No one said a word. They just looked at me.

"What did you see, Hunk?" I moved over to him.

He never budged. But he answered, looking straight up. "A person."

"When?"

"When we turned the corner."

I didn't really believe him. I figured he was parroting my words, from earlier.

"Where?"

"Up on that metal bridge." But I'd said that, too.

"Doing what?"

"Holding a big piece of pipe." I'd said that, too.

"What did he look like?" I hadn't said that.

"He had long white hair," Hunk answered. "And he was dressed in rags."

Everyone looked at me, waiting for me to shake my head no.

I couldn't.

"Is that what you saw, too?" Cherry asked.

I still played it down. "I'm not sure." I stood up to look around. I suddenly felt very uneasy, and everyone else looked that way, too.

Hunk made it even worse. "He was putting those pipes on the tracks," he said to the ceiling. "He wanted us to crash. He was trying to kill us."

Silence. Everyone just waited.

"You guys stay close," I said, finally. "I'm going to have a look around. Try to get Hunk in shape, so we can get moving if we have to."

"Don't go off alone," Mary said.

"I'm just going to figure out where we are. You guys stick close," I repeated.

I walked off a little way, just over to the train wreckage. I looked up at the catwalk again. He had been up there. He wasn't there now, but he had been. I could see him again as clearly as if he were standing right there. That tortured, strange face with those spastic movements.

I followed the catwalk with my eyes. I tried to

imagine where he could have gone—or come from. The catwalk spanned the tunnel. It was an overpass. It could lead anywhere.

I kept trying to figure out where this area was, or what it was. I had the four sheets of the map yet, but I couldn't be sure anymore after that ride. The tracks weren't even indicated on the chart. Maybe they had been installed since the map had been drawn.

It was hot here. There were lots of doors and chambers and things that looked like steam pipes with gauges. I'd never seen so many handwheels in my life—big ones and tiny ones and some that looked as if they could open the sluice gates of Niagara Falls. There was a steady turbine sound above me, which seemed strange. All the pipes ran up, too—and the network of wheels and gauges on the ceiling seemed to indicate that this was the lower level of something with a lot of machines and works.

There was a telephone on the wall in a cage, some kind of utility phone like the private lines to the police that you see on expressway ramps, and in parks. It had the single word OFFICE underneath the cage.

I suddenly understood exactly where we were.

I went back to the group, who were just waiting.

"I think I know where we are."

"Where?" Cherry asked.

"You're not going to believe it."

They looked at one another; they couldn't imagine.

"Underneath the plant," I said.

They still didn't get it—not even Mary.

"The waste-water treatment plant. I think we're right underneath. That would explain the train, too. It's some kind of shuttle that runs to and from the plant."

"Well, where is everyone?" Krevitch asked.

"Upstairs," I said. "This is like the basement—or the sub-basement. Everything's probably a couple stories up. Besides, it's the weekend."

"So how do we get out of here?" Cherry said.

"There's a phone right over there on the wall."

"A phone?"

"Some kind of in-house thing. All we've got to do is pick it up."

I looked at Mary. I knew what she was thinking. "I guess that would be your father, huh?"

"Probably," she answered. "It doesn't matter, though. He'd find out anyway. . . ." Krevitch glanced nervously over at the wrecked train. So did Cherry.

"Remember," Cherry said, "we were on a tour, and we got lost."

"They know better than that," Mary said. "They're the ones who give the tours."

"We came in for a tour permit," Cherry persisted, "and took the wrong turn."

We all looked at the train again.

"We'll probably get fined," Krevitch said. "Or sued by the city."

"If we do, we do," I answered.

"Even put in jail," he continued. His voice was all quivers.

"And kicked out of Journalism," Cherry added. "And suspended from school. . . ." She looked at Mary. "And I hate to think of what your old man's going to do to you."

Mary looked as though she hated to think about it, too.

"I still say we ought to go with the accident story," Cherry said. "A wrong turn . . ."

I was trying to think, too. Lies, alibis—some escape route. "Hunk," I said, "how do you feel now?"

"Fine," he answered in his peculiar new voice.

"Can you get up?"

"Sure." But he didn't move.

I got down on one side of him, and Krevitch on the other.

"I don't need any help," he said, and got up— suddenly—with no support at all. It was frightening, though, to watch the way he rose—like Lazarus, from the dead. It didn't look remotely natural, or even possible. He stood there like a living corpse, with dried blood the color of coffee on his ears and nose and teeth. He didn't even have the old Hunk posture, ape-like and loose. He stood very straight, with his head up and his fingertips just touching.

"Are you sure . . . ?" I asked.

"Sure."

We all looked at each other as if maybe, after

all, we might get out and away. But just then he shook his head—a violent, quick shake as though he were tossing off a hat. He did it just once, but in that instant you could see the old Hunk—the eyes, the expression—everything. Then that new thing oozed back, and he stood there, a stranger.

No.

"We'd better use the phone," I said. "We need help."

No one argued. We all walked over to that little cage I'd discovered. Even Hunk. On the way, Krevitch made one last try.

"We can say it was a fraternity stunt," he said, "and they forced us down here, to stay the night." But no one picked it up, not even Cherry.

"Krevitch," I said, tapping the cage, "it's locked." That's all you ever needed to say to Krevitch. One hand went immediately to his back pocket, and out came his little kit—soggy, but still intact. He examined the cage for a second, took a tiny L-shaped tool out of the package, inserted it into the lock, and twisted.

It opened right up.

"Thank you," I said. Krevitch didn't even answer. He just did the strange little triumphant strut he'd always do after picking a lock—a kind of ritual in which he'd circle all of us, smiling proudly, with his ears beet red.

I stared at the receiver a second.

"Who wants to do the talking?" I asked. No one made a move.

I picked up the phone. I listened. There was

nothing for a moment, like on the house phone of a hotel.

Then there was a connection.

"Malgren."

I cupped the receiver. "It's your father," I whispered. The look on Mary's face was total helplessness. Her color drained as I watched. Everyone else looked pretty helpless, too.

"Malgren!" the voice repeated.

I still didn't talk. I had the most terrible dread suddenly. A real sinking in my guts.

"Who the fuck is this?"

I guess we all did it together. Four hands reached out and pushed down the cradle. Then—amazingly—a fifth. Hunk's.

I hung up the phone.

"We'll figure a way out ourselves," Mary said, her voice trembling. "Come on."

She actually pulled me away, still shaking.

Eighteen

We've got to go up." Cherry said. "We can't just keep going on. We've got to go up!" She actually stared up into the air, as if there might be a trapdoor or hatch in the ceiling. We'd been walking along the tunnel for ten minutes or so, getting nowhere. She was starting to lose her grip. Maybe we all were.

We kept following those utility lights blindly. We passed two doors. Both times we stopped and picked the locks, and both times we missed. One was a boiler room, and one was a storage closet for chemicals and supplies. We found thick metal containers of compressed chlorine gas, and hundred-pound sacks of a *polymer*-something, and kegs of rivets, and welding masks, and huge cans of oil, and complicated, bizarre machinery, but no exit. No staircase, no corridor—nothing.

"There!" Cherry said suddenly. She'd said that at the doors of the boiler room and the storage closet too, so we didn't get too excited. But this time there did seem to be something. It was a big metal door, with a little wired-glass circle in it.

"An elevator!" she cried.

It was. It seemed incredible, down here. But then, so did the phone, and even the light bulbs. It was some kind of archaic loading device, black and battered and greasy.

"Go ahead," she said, as always.

I opened the door—the first one we'd run across down here that wasn't locked. Then a gate. But I didn't step inside. It was pitch black. I reached in, stretching, and flicked a couple switches and pushed a couple buttons.

"There's no power," I said. I was almost relieved.

"Krevitch," Cherry said, "turn this goddamned thing on."

Krevitch stepped forward with his kit. He got as close to those buttons as he could without actually stepping inside the dark chamber. Cherry held the flashlight so he could see. The flashlight kept dimming and she kept shaking it, violently, while poor Krevitch flinched and searched for a power button or keyhole.

He found a slot.

He found a corresponding tool in his kit.

He inserted it. He bent it a little. Nothing.

He tried another one. This time, light—or a light—flickered. The more he jiggled, the more it flickered, and finally the light—a small bulb on the ceiling—stayed on. But very weakly and oddly, almost as if it were shorted. For the first time after a triumph, little Krevitch refrained from his dance. He peered up at the bulb doubtfully.

"I know now," Cherry said, and stepped boldly

into the car. It creaked a little, with her weight. None of us followed.

"Come *on*," she said, but we all stood rooted to the spot, as if a sixth sense were operating. "All we do is shut the gate. Once the gate is shut, the power goes on. I remember one like this from my uncle's surplus store. They use it to haul freight. *Come on!*"

Her shout echoed. It made us all look up into the darkness of the chute and cables, as if someone might hear.

We got on finally, one by one. Five bodies, and all that weight.

"Stand clear," she said, whispering this time. She slammed the gate shut. Then the door.

Nothing happened, except that the little light went out.

"Oh, Jesus Christ," she said in the darkness. I could hear her fumbling with the flashlight again. It wouldn't go on. I could hear everyone breathing—feel everyone breathing. Everything seemed so close in the dark. She hit someone—maybe Hunk—shaking the flashlight, but finally she had a flicker. She swung the light up into position—right in my eyes. Then on the control panel.

Krevitch peered at that little slot again. "I know that's for the key," he said. He went at it with the same tool. The little light glimmered again, but it wouldn't stay on. Then the strangest thing of all happened. Cherry pressed a white button while Krevitch was jiggling in that slot—and the elevator suddenly began to move.

Down. With a sigh—as though air was escaping from something hydraulic. No power at all, just that regular, easy, gentle descent. It was that same horrible feeling of the coasting train. . . .

"Oh, no . . . ," Mary said. We all watched the cement and metal shaft passing as we fell noiselessly, easily. A huge weight rose right before our eyes—about a foot away—maybe a kind of balance, or pendulum.

We came to rest with a gentle bump in the dark. There wasn't even a flicker in the ceiling light.

"Piss!" Cherry said. "Can you get it back up?"

Krevitch tried and tried. His eyes were red, and he was squinting and sweating and peering and grunting—sighing and scratching, pushing and bending those little tools until the slot was jimmied completely out of shape. But he couldn't make the connection.

"There must be another elevator," I said. "Or a staircase."

We pulled open the gate. Then the door. It was dark down here, but not black—unless my eyes were just getting used to it all. It was an older section, with a lower overhead—and humid. The air was thick and warm, almost like a swamp. There was another telephone in another cage on the wall, just like the one upstairs.

We all looked at it, and then at one another, exactly as we'd done earlier. And we all walked away from it just as fast.

I think I was the first one to figure out where we were. "Bricks," I said, pointing to the walls.

No one seemed to make the connection.

"We're in the Catacombs. This is what we were trying to find earlier."

But no one really seemed to care now. Earlier seemed like years ago.

"Let's find a goddamned door," Cherry said. She took the lead with the flashlight. There was rubble in the pathway, as though this area hadn't been used in years. There were big fans of bricks set into the wall, almost like something medieval. There were old clay pipe sections and something that looked like a small silo, built from the floor right up through the ceiling. It was giving off terrific heat.

"The sludge oven," I guessed. But no one cared.

"Here," Cherry said.

"An elevator?"

"No . . . ," She didn't say what. She just stood in front of it. We had to look ourselves. It was a door, but it wasn't a door—at least, not one that had been opened in years. It was blackish, and flaked with corrosion. It looked like something out of another century, with huge rusty hinges and a crossbar. It had that same framework of bricks around the top, as if it had once been a passage or entranceway.

"The manhole looked this way too," Cherry said, when she saw the doubt on our faces. "Remember? All rusted. It's probably the way out.

She still had her crowbar. I was amazed. The duffle bag was one of the few things she'd managed to hang on to through it all. She began to pry. Rusted metal flaked away easily, like old clay. She gave the bar a smash, and that loosened too. She gave it another smash, and the thing broke right in two, as if it were made of soft stone. I never saw such determination on anyone's face. We all hit the duffle bag and started prying and poking with whatever came to hand—harpoons, screwdrivers, a hammer, a penknife. The noise was incredible—echoes and clangs and the constant peppering sound of bits and pieces of metal hitting the ground.

"Okay," she said to Hunk. He seemed to understand immediately, bandaged head and all. He stepped forward, a little shakily, but Hunk all the way. He gave the thing a good yank.

"Almost," Cherry said, and we all went to work again.

Krevitch used the hammer. Mary was giving it everything she had with the handle of her harpoon. I was using a hammer and a screwdriver at once, and Cherry was knocking off about two pounds of corroded metal with every swing of her crowbar. It was like breaking into a tomb.

"It's coming!" she said, prying at a space that grew with each heave of the crowbar. "I just hope to hell this leads somewhere!"

Cherry stepped back, and Hunk gave it another go—or tried to. He had to stop a second to give his head one of those terrible shakes. Then another.

Then everything seemed cleared, or uncleared, and he grabbed the open edge of that door with both hands and pulled—pulled like a maniac—pulled so hard and with such fury that he terrified all of us. It was like some prehistoric man wrestling with a rock.

It gave. The way the door opened was like something out of a horror film. One of the three old creaking hinges broke right off. Then we all helped Hunk pull, and kept pulling until we had the thing half open.

"What is it?" Krevitch asked. We were blocking his view.

"It's hard to tell," I said. It was. It was darker—unless every new path and tunnel and turnoff down there always seemed darker and more hopeless than the last. But there was something else, too.

At first I didn't quite get it, maybe because I'd been saturated with gas and sewage for the past few hours.

Mary picked it right out. "What's that smell?" she asked, sniffing.

We all began to sniff and look.

"Smoke?" I guessed.

"Meat," Krevitch said.

That was it. It smelled like a roast. Beef. Such an impossible smell, coming from down here. It was unmistakable now. My mouth began to water.

"Maybe it's just chemicals or something," Krevitch said. "Like a mirage, only a smell. . . ."

"Or maybe we're underneath a restaurant," Cherry tried.

"Well . . . ?" I asked. But we all just stood there.

"Let's go," Cherry said. "At least we're out of the pipes. Any passage is bound to lead up."

"Okay." I took the flashlight, or what was left of the flashlight, gave it a couple whacks and cracks, and led the way. A little of the old Five-Star optimism was back.

Krevitch even managed to make a joke. "If it is meat," he said, twitching, "maybe they'll ask us to stay for dinner!"

Nineteen

Krevitch wasn't that far off. There was someone living in there. Mary picked it up again, right away. All I saw were piles of rocks and rags and assorted boards, but Mary found designs.

"That's a shelf," she said.

And it was. When you looked carefully, you could see it—a crude makeshift shelf, or some kind of cupboard. The concrete blocks stacked in the corner formed a little table. The rusty tuna can turned out to hold a wick made of a twisted rag, set in oil. There was a large collection of scrap bottles and pipes and paper and rags, all piled neatly in the middle of the floor as if someone was storing the objects for future use.

Someone living there right now.

The cooking smell grew stronger. It seemed to unnerve Krevitch completely, as if maybe he really had expected to discover the back end of a Howard Johnson's.

"What the hell?" he asked, sniffing. He looked around wildly at the boards and rocks, and at that pile of junk.

"Relax, Krevitch. It's probably just some hobo,"

I said. But he really was upset, as if we were finally caught in the eye of a long, hopeless whirlpool.

"We're never going to get out of this goddamn place!" he shrieked. It was horrible— even for Krevitch. His face, voice—nothing even seemed close to the Krevitch we knew. "I don't care about my camera!" he shouted—the first time I'd even thought of the camera. "I don't care about the train! I don't care about school—I don't care about anything! I just want to get out of this fucking place!"

I had to grab him. "Krevitch!"

"*What?*"

"Stop screaming! We will get out of here!"

"We will?" he asked in the most childish voice, and with the most puzzled expression. He stood there looking up at me, while I held each of his shaking, skinny shoulders.

"Of course we will." But his look threw me, that pathetic, quivering face. Suddenly I was wondering myself. . . .

"Come on," I said. "Hang in there." I sort of pushed him forward, through the room.

And into another. And another. A series of rooms, with open ends of long pipes exposed, gaping, as if the place had once been some kind of settling pool, or a series of pools or chambers.

Cherry started theorizing, loudly, as though she was trying to convince herself. "Hoboes," she said, "or maybe kids. Kids love places like this. They come down here on weekends. You know. It's like playing house." She stopped at an overturned nail keg which someone had been using as a stool.

"What about the guy with the white hair?" Krevitch asked.

No one answered.

"It's five against one," I finally said, but that didn't seem to reassure anyone too much. Krevitch especially. He started trembling all over again. I actually had to steer him along.

"We have to get out of here," he said for the hundredth time.

"Then keep walking."

There was a big pile of rags and brush and even something that looked like furniture stuffing, covered with gunny sacks. The bed? It had the same look as everything else—so primitive that you couldn't quite believe it had been used by anyone half-civilized, or even in his right mind.

There were some crude utensils hooked on the wall—a knife of scrap metal, and two or three small spears made of construction rods with sharpened tips.

In a hole surrounded by chunks of cement there was a fire. It was lit. Someone had been here and fled. Or was still here and hiding. There was an old, blackened piece of metal grating over the fire, exactly like the grating of the manhole cap we'd seen earlier. There was something on top of the grating, cooking in a discolored ham tin. It wasn't ham. It was hard to tell what it was—something small, like a rabbit or chicken. It was burnt black.

"We interrupted someone," Mary said. "They left it."

Krevitch leaned over it, staring. None of us had eaten in a long time. He really did look hungry.

"What is it?" he asked.

"Some kind of meat," Mary answered.

"But what?"

I could see it clearly now. I didn't have the nerve to say it.

Cherry did. "Jesus Christ. It's a rat!"

That did it. Krevitch cracked. "A rat?" It wasn't his voice at all. It wasn't his face. He began to jump—almost like a little trapped rat himself. He smashed right into the wall.

"This is crazy!" he screamed. "There's something crazy down here! Eating rats! Dumping pipes on us!" He ripped the scrap-metal knife down off the wall. He began to wave it wildly. He walked to all the different corners. He walked back to us. He walked around us. He just missed me with that knife.

"I'm getting out of here right now!" he screamed.

"Krevitch—shut up! We're all going to get out of here!"

He didn't hear a word. He didn't see me. He really was alone now—completely—tiny and powerless, waving a knife.

He suddenly broke into a run—and there was no place to run. He crashed into that same wall with the utensils again. A spear came clattering down. He hit another wall. He seemed to be having a fit, or convulsions. The mouth of a large pipe opened up right into the wall. He suddenly scurried into that, like an escaping animal, on his hands and knees.

"Krevitch!"

No answer. He all but disappeared from sight. All we could see were his heels. We could hear the metal of his knife blade scraping the pipe. There was gasping—and crying—horrible echoes from inside, funneled back loud and clear.

"Krevitch—you'll get lost in there!"

"I'm getting out of here!" he answered from deep inside. None of us followed. We gathered around outside the mouth of the pipe.

"Krevitch," I called in again.

This time he took longer to answer. When he finally did, his voice sounded as though it was coming from far off in another room.

"Hey," he called. "It turns!"

Then nothing else for a moment.

Then a horrible scream.

"Krevitch!"

He just kept screaming. There was the sound of something—fighting or scuffling—deep inside the pipe.

I crawled in fast, with the crowbar and the flashlight. The rest crawled in after me, none of us thinking of anything but Krevitch. The screaming and the scuffling continued—horribly close, suddenly, inside the pipe. The pipe was old glazed clay, and filthy. You could hear and actually feel metal and bodies—parts of bodies—striking the pipe sides. You could still hear Krevitch screaming—and someone else, too, grunting and gasping.

"Help!" Krevitch shrieked horribly.

"We're coming!" I crawled as I'd never crawled in my life. There was the turn he'd just described, and beyond that, an opening. At the end of the opening was a concrete tank. On the edge of the tank was Krevitch—on his back—struggling with someone, all rags and white hair. The man was right on top of him, with a long iron construction rod raised over his body.

Krevitch gave one last terrrible scream as the spear went down into him. Then the man pulled the rod out and plunged it in again.

I shouted—something—anything—at the top of my lungs. I was still crawling. I threw my crowbar as far as it would go, through the opening. I threw the flashlight. Nothing reached him, but the crowbar chipped off an edge of the pipe and spun wildly, making a clatter.

The man looked up—surprised. He stared at me for just a second. Then he began to run—that same crippled, spastic loping as earlier—waving the spear. He staggered along the edge of the tank until he came to some up-ended concrete pipe sections in the water. He jumped onto those and disappeared on the other side of the tank.

When I turned around, Krevitch was standing up, with everyone around him, staring. I don't think any of us believed it, even with the blood.

"Are you hurt?" I asked, completely out of breath.

"He is," Mary said.

"I'm all right," Krevitch answered

He wasn't. He toppled right over, onto Hunk. He was all blood. Hunk eased him down to the ground as gently as he could. Every time Krevitch breathed, blood poured out of wounds in his chest and in his stomach. Thick blood, and dark. All we could think of was to hold him down, so that he wouldn't move.

Mary pressed the last of her dress against the wounds, and Cherry was rummaging in her pants pocket for something to use. But none of it was worth much. Krevitch just kept on gasping and staring right through us.

The spear must have hit his heart or his lungs. In about three minutes he stopped moving and breathing completely.

Twenty

"The telephone."

I don't think I said more than that. I don't think I thought more than that. We had to get back to the telephone—the one we'd just passed, by the elevator. Now.

"Krevitch . . . ," Mary said hopelessly.

"He's dead. Come on!"

We left him there. We crawled back into the pipe. None of us looked back. None of us said a word. I don't think we even breathed heavily, as before. We just crawled.

We made our way back through those rooms the same way. We didn't look left or right. I usually have a poor sense of direction, but I found every corridor and every little room, exactly as earlier: the stove with the cooked rat, the piles of rags and brush covered with burlap, the cans of oil with rag wicks. We walked right by the last of our own gear, which we'd left lying on the floor. I grabbed one knapsack in passing. Everyone kept pace, even Hunk.

We came out at that battered medieval door. I

went left, as though it was my own house. Even when I wasn't sure, I was sure. Instinctively.

There was the elevator. There was the telephone.

The cage of the phone was locked, just as the first one had been. I'd forgotten about that. The tools were all in Krevitch's back pocket.

Hunk stood right behind me, breathing calmly.

"Hunk," I said, meaning "give it a smash." But when I looked at him, he had that same suspended look again. And Cherry too. Both of them completely drained of color, or any kind of expression.

Mary too.

I found a brick and went at it myself. It took only two or three good swings before it opened up. The others all watched, like an audience.

I picked up the receiver.

"He might be gone," Mary said.

I checked my watch. It was after five. "Someone would be there, wouldn't they?"

"I don't know."

I waited, listening to that blankness and breathing hard into the receiver.

"*Malgren.*"

"Mr. Malgren," I began without a pause. "This is Tom."

"*Who?*"

"Tom Marsh—Mary's friend."

There was a terrible pause. You could actually picture him trying to figure it. The rest were looking at me as if they could picture it, too.

"Where are you?" His voice was deadly. He knew we were somewhere in the pipes. That's where these phones connected.

"We're down in the sewer. I came down here with Mary and a couple people from school."

There was that same silence again.

"Mary?"

"We came down here to do a story for the paper."

"I told you—" he began again. But then he stopped. Something funny was happening to his breathing. It sounded weak and flutey, almost as if he were having an attack. He actually dropped the phone. You could hear him fumbling to pick it up again, and coughing.

"Mr. Malgren," I said, when I was sure he had the phone back in place, "we've had some trouble. We were attacked. One of our friends was killed."

"Killed?"

"Yes."

He didn't seem as surprised as you'd think he'd be. After a moment, he asked, *"Where are you?"*

"I don't know exactly. Somewhere underneath—"

"What's the number of the phone box?"

I had to look. There was a yellow stenciled number sprayed underneath the cage.

"Five."

There was another long pause, as if he were trying to visualize the location of Five.

"Five?"

"Yes."

He paused again, and asked the strangest question. *"Have you talked to anyone else up here?"*

"No."

"Was that you who called earlier and hung up?"

"Yes."

"Does anyone eles know you went down there?"

"No," I answered, not understanding.

"From school or anywhere?"

"No."

"Did you run into anyone else down there?"

"Just the person who attacked us. Mr. Malgren, we really need—"

"Now listen!" he said. His voice had that tremor again. *"I'm coming down there. It'll take maybe ten minutes. I want you to hang up the phone and leave it hung up. Even if it rings—don't pick it up. If you run into anyone, don't say a word. Just keep quiet and wait for me. Stay right there by the phone. Understand?"*

"Yes," I said.

"When I come down there, I want to find you right there by the elevator."

"All right."

"How many of you are there?"

"Four."

"And the fifth one's been murdered?"

"Yes. Krevitch." I think that was the first time that the word really hit me, when someone else said it. Krevitch had been murdered.

"And you saw who did it?"

"Yes."

You could hear his breath catch again, and the hesitant breathing. *"Do you know who it was?"*

"Some crazy person. Dressed in rags, with white hair."

Silence. I figured he was thinking about that. Finally he said, *"All right. Do what I said. I'm on my way."*

"Are you going to bring the police?" I asked. "Or a doctor? Hunk's—"

"Do exactly what I said!" he repeated. Then he hung up. Just that dead line again—no dial tone, nothing.

I turned back to the group. They all looked just as numb as before.

"He's on his way," I said. There should have been some relief then, but everyone was too drained. We were all filthy and covered with blood. Mary's face was the most horrible I'd ever seen it—as if she'd died herself. Her lips were pale and trembling, and her eyes looked terrified. She clasped both her arms around her own body. She hardly had any of her clothes left on. I tried to hold her to stop her from shaking, but it was like holding a stranger.

"It'll be better now," I said, but that only brought on more trembling. I tried to think of something she could wear. The knapsack had the lunch in it, and one of her own small checkered tablecloths from home. I helped her wrap that around herself, and gave her my belt. She couldn't stop trembling, though, and that terrified look never left her face.

Hunk and Cherry just wandered in circles, like zombies. It was as if we were all waiting for execution.

The knapsack lay open on the ground. You could see the food—crushed sandwiches, and carrot cake, and some cut-up bell peppers and celery, all in little plastic bags. There were some small bottles of fruit juice, too.

I was almost ashamed to think of it, but I was hungry.

I was going to ask them, then I wasn't.

Then I did.

"Is anyone hungry?"

They all looked at me as if I were insane. But then they started wandering over closer to the knapsack, and within a couple minutes we were all stuffing ourselves—gorging. We finished off everything in that bag—the fruit, sandwiches, hard-boiled eggs, everything—like starving people. Food was actually falling from our mouths as we stuffed it in. It was the first time I could ever remember all of us finishing one of Mary's expedition lunches—and we were one short. We would have eaten more, if there had been more. We never said a word to one another. We just ate.

Twenty-one

The empty elevator came alive. It was strange to see its light go on behind the gates, and to suddenly hear and feel the power of the motor, after all that silence. It was like something haunted. The door closed on its own and it rose, still empty.

We got up and stood around the outside of the shaft in a half-circle. You could hear it come to a stop far above.

You could hear him get on.

Then it came down again.

The doors opened. He stared at us through the gate. He was wearing his uniform, and a leather jacket with a fur collar. He was holding a shotgun. He took us all in, one by one, and when those sad dark eyes met mine, I knew what I'd known every time I'd ever looked at Mr. Malgren. He hated me. I'd never known why, but he hated me.

"Hello," I said weakly, as he opened the gate. It echoed and sounded ridiculous.

He didn't answer. He just stepped out, limping. He kept taking us all in. His eyes didn't rest on

Mary any longer than they rested on the others.
The gun was half-cradled in his arm, pointing at
me.

"Did you bring anyone with you?" I asked.

He still didn't answer. He was looking so ominous now that the others actually started to back
up. Mary was all but hiding behind Cherry.

Finally he asked, "Is there anyone else down
here with you?"

"Just Krevitch," I answered. "And he's dead."

"Where?"

"On the other side. Through some pipes. I can
show you."

He didn't answer. He looked around silently,
thinking—exactly the way I'd imagined him during all those pauses on the phone. He didn't ask if
any of us were hurt, sick—nothing.

"How long have you been down here?" he finally said.

"Since morning. About eleven."

"And you didn't meet anyone all day?" Exactly
what he'd asked me earlier.

"No."

He took a slow look around again, as if there
might be an accomplice hiding behind the pipes.

"And you didn't call out on any other phones?"

"No." I couldn't figure out why he was asking
these questions. "Hunk's hurt," I said. "He needs
a doctor. Did you call the police or anyone?"

He still wouldn't answer. He shined his flashlight into a far corner. He caught a rat's red eyes.

He looked at it casually, as if he was used to that. He flashed the light into a few other areas.

"How did you get down here in this section?" he asked.

"We got on a train. It went wild. It wouldn't stop."

He studied my face hard. I had the distinct feeling he'd blast my head off with that shotgun, if he could.

"The pipe shuttle? What were you doing over there?"

"That's where we came in."

He looked at Mary. He looked at me. He looked at all of us, as if he was trying to put pieces together. I didn't want to lie to him. I didn't want to do anything but stop talking and just get out of there.

"Describe this . . . person," he said.

"Kind of short, with stringy white hair, and dressed in rags."

He glanced around, but the others didn't have anything to add.

"Did you get a close look?" he continued.

"Maybe fifteen feet away."

Again that long pause. He was the only person I ever met who thought like that—stopping dead and standing stiffly. And every time his look came back to us, there was the same sullen expression in his eyes.

He still hadn't said a word to Mary.

"Where's the body?" he asked me.

"It's all the way back. Through an old door we

broke open, then an unused section—then through some pipes."

"An old door?"

"It looked like it hadn't been used in years."

"Show me."

"I think that's where the person is living," I warned.

"Show me," he said again, adjusting the shotgun.

"Mr. Malgren," I said, "don't you think we should get out of here first—and come back later with the police? Krevitch is already dead, and Hunk is hurt bad."

"Show me—goddammit!" he suddenly shouted. "Don't tell me what to do! You're trespassing on city property! I could blast your heads off right now! You show me that goddamned door!"

This time he really did point the gun at me.

"Where is it?" he repeated.

I turned around. Both of the women were cowering behind Hunk.

"Show him," Mary said.

"All right," I answered. "This way."

He waited until we'd all gotten in front of him. Then he said, "Go ahead."

None of us spoke another word. We just walked.

Twenty-two

Mr. Malgren stood in front of that old corroded door a long time. He was studying it. He shook his head once or twice, as if something puzzled him. He looked over and around and on all sides of the door.

"I've passed by this thing a hundred times . . . ," he said, more to himself than to us. I looked at Cherry and Mary, and they were both looking at me. There was something going on inside his head which none of us knew anything about, not even his own daughter. You could tell, just by the way his eyes searched for the slightest detail. . . .

The same thing happened the second we were inside those bizarre living quarters again.

"He might have come back," I warned, but Mr. Malgren didn't seem to care. He was ready for it. He walked into the chamber with his shotgun, as though he owned the place.

"Did you find anything when you were in here before?" he asked—the first time he'd addressed me since the gun threat.

"Like what?"

"*Anything*—identification—anything!" He never looked at me. He seemed to be making it a point not to look at any of us.

"No," I answered.

"That's all I wanted to know."

He studied the piles of bricks and bottles and stones, which had been stacked up at little intervals. He studied—very carefully—the pile of rags and brush in the corner, which made up the bed. He even got down on one knee to look more closely. He picked up something in his fingers: a long strand of white hair.

"I've been looking for this," he said—more to himself, again, than to us. I remembered the disappearance of the company engineer, but it still seemed peculiar. *I*, not we. And the obsessive look on his face. Herding us all around with a shotgun. I had the same feeling I'd had in his kitchen, when he'd reacted so strangely to my questions. Something ran deeper. He was afraid.

He started to search every corner now, even though I could see that it hurt him to walk. He studied the burnt rat, and the sticks and spears in the makeshift kitchen. He searched carefully behind the concrete blocks and the pipe sections. He found some other supplies that we hadn't noticed in a wooden box against the wall: pieces of cloth, and plastic bags, and odd bits of junk and hardware.

I pointed to the pipe. "We went through there."

He looked at the gaping mouth in the wall, but he didn't move toward it. If he'd been at home, I would have said he was drunk. He looked dazed, or lost in memory. The more he found, the more he wanted to find. He started poking around in a pile of refuse—boards and cans and pieces of rubber and plastic—junk that someone might have gathered by the armload from one of the filter traps out in the tanks. He found another small alcove we'd overlooked, and he began to search around in there.

"What's he looking for?" Cherry whispered, when he was out of earshot. I didn't know. Mary didn't know. And Hunk just continued to give his head those periodic, violent shakes.

I got curious myself. He looked so worried, so involved. I let my eyes wander over the higher places. There was a series of small squares up near the ceiling, like the crenellations in a castle wall, where the bricks were set alternately. I could see within them easily, because of my height. Anyone else would probably have overlooked them. Some of the squares were empty, and some were stuffed with straw and lint, as if rodents were nesting there. Some of them were jammed with pieces of metal and bits of wood and odd material—old pens, matchbooks, cardboard—as if the hermit had stashed them away up high himself, for later use.

I looked carefully. Cotton. Old razor blades. A few damaged combs, and pins. One of the cubicles had what looked like a tiny bundle of papers. I reached up and took them down. They actually began to disintegrate in my hand. They were mostly old can labels, collected and bound with a piece of string. The top one had writing on the blank side—a wild, almost illegible scrawl. The light was terrible, but I could read a couple of the words, damage and all.

before I go crazy

I almost said "Look" out loud. Something checked me. I stuffed the little bundle into my pocket.

Just in time, too. Mr. Malgren came back in from the other room.

"You find anything?" he asked.

"Just junk." I pointed to a rat's nest.

He looked at me so hard that for a second I was sure he must have seen me. But then he stared at Cherry and Mary and Hunk just as hard.

"What's the matter with him?" he asked, pointing to Hunk as if Hunk couldn't hear at all.

"He hit his head when the train piled up."

Hunk nodded. I thought he was going to try to say something. But instead, he just gave his head a jerk.

"It's probably did him good," Mr. Malgren said. "He's an idiot anyway, isn't he?"

Something froze up in Hunk, right in the middle of his head-shake. You could see the old Hunk eyes. Cherry moved over toward him, and so did Mary, in case Hunk reacted. Mr. Malgren didn't seem to notice. He shook his head a little sadly, as if he were dealing with defectives.

"Can we go get Krevitch now?" I asked.

He shook his head at me sadly, as if I were the idiot. "Where did you leave him?"

"Right through that pipe. On the cement landing."

"By the tank?" he asked. I could see he knew the area.

"Yes."

"And you expect him to still be there?"

That confused me. Where could he go?

"Do you know what's in that water?" he asked.

Then I understood. "It was only a half-hour ago," I tried.

"You couldn't leave anything dead in there five minutes," he answered. "Not even half-dead."

I was having a hard time breathing. All I could see was Krevitch lying there, neatly, on the cement ledge where Hunk and I had tried to arrange him a little.

Mr. Malgren laughed at the looks on all of our faces.

"All right," he said. "You want to go see? We'll go see."

Suddenly I didn't want to go see at all. None of us did.

"Let's go," he repeated. He raised the gun. "You first," motioning me down on my hands and knees, into the pipe. "You're such a good leader. Lead!"

I crawled in. It was almost familiar to me now. Cherry followed, and Hunk was behind her. That left Mary, way in back with her father. I hadn't crawled ten feet before I heard a terrible round of slapping. Mary cried out—so loudly that I instinctively shot up, smashing my head against the top of the sewer pipe. It was hard to turn around to look, but I did—past Cherry and past Hunk. Mary was at the entrance of the pipe, and her father was slapping her with one hand—hard—first left, then right.

"Just like your mother!" he was shouting. "A liar and a sneak! A liar"—and he slapped her—"and a sneak!" He kept repeating "liar" and "sneak," slapping her on each word. My head was splitting and I could barely see, but I still wanted to crawl back to her. Cherry stopped me.

"Keep moving!" she ordered. "He's lost his mind!"

I still tried to edge my way by her, back to Mary. This time Cherry actually struck me on the shoulders with her fist, as if she was losing her own mind.

"If you want to live," she said, "keep moving." The look on her face was unbelievable. I'd never seen Cherry terrified before.

"All right," I answered. I turned toward the pool again and kept crawling.

Twenty-three

He was right.

Krevitch's body was gone. The blood was still on the concrete, thick and solid as liver, but all you could trace beyond that was a slippery trail, leading right over the ledge and into the water. There were wet paw prints all over the cement, and larger blurry patches of water.

"That's from walking backwards," Mr. Malgren said, studying those wet patches, "when they dragged the body in." He peered at all of us, one by one. He seemed to enjoy the incredulous expressions on our faces. He pulled up one pants leg. There was a huge stained bandage wrapped around the calf.

"You wanted to know what's down here? And what they do?" He rubbed the wound a little, almost as if enoying that, too. He looked over at the coagulated blood on the cement, and at the trail leading into the pool. "That's what's down here, and that's what they do."

He limped over to the edge of the pool, with the shotgun ready. He gazed down into the muck. "It's the only place down here that's warm enough for them," he said. "You find them in the other sections once in a while, but they're dead, from the cold and chemicals. This is the only section where they do just fine. . . ."

Hunk asked, "Alligators?" He was just beginning to make the connection; you could actually see him straining to think. It was pathetic, but Mr. Malgren seemed to enjoy that, too.

"That's right, Mr. Hunk," he mocked. "Old Florida alligators. The kind you used to buy at the pet stores."

"I never had an alligator," Hunk answered. "Just a turtle. And some tropical fish. I've still got my turtle. He's fourteen years old now. Juniper."

"Mr. Malgren," Cherry began, staring at the blood. She looked very sick.

"Don't interrupt," Mr. Malgren answered without even glancing at her. "I'm having a deep philosophical discussion with your friend, Mr. Hunk. All you people from City University have such deep philosophical ideas. . . ." He smiled terribly.

"I'm not from the University," Hunk interjected, with an earnest look on his face. "I just mow the lawns over there."

"Mr. Malgren," Cherry tried again.

"I said, don't interrupt!" He turned around and pointed the shotgun at her. For a minute, Cherry just stared. Then she did something I'd only seen her do once before, during that homecoming fiasco when she'd discovered the joke. She started to cry. Her shoulders shook and her face contorted and she stuffed her hands over her mouth and began to gag and choke—a real sobbing.

Mr. Malgren laughed. "Another deep philosopher," he said, over her hacking. "Does anyone else have anything to add? I know you university students have a lot of intellectual ideas."

Mary was crying now, too. I didn't know what to do. Mr. Malgren was taking it all in with a kind of glee, so much so that when his face suddenly straightened out and he asked me something, I didn't get it at all.

"What?" I asked.

"Where did he go?" he repeated.

"Who?"

"White hair and rags—asshole—when he ran!"

"Oh . . . ," I said. It took me that long. Cherry's wailing was reverberating horribly, wall to wall. I couldn't even think. I had to shout.

"Over there." I pointed to one of those up-ended concrete sections in the pool. "He ran across them."

He turned to look. There was a rounded structure like a miniature gas-store tank up beyond the pool. There was a handrail around it. I could almost see white hair and rags taking that route. It was the only possible place to run.

"Let's go," he said.

I thought he meant go back. Everyone else probably did too, because Cherry stopped choking immediately, and Hunk stepped forward, and even Mary looked alive again suddenly.

But then he motioned us all in the other direction, toward the pool.

"We're going to make a little search," he said. "For our friend."

Cherry's face went blank. From tears to relief to total surprise again. That's when she cracked.

"I'm going back," she said. That's all. Then she actually turned around, toward the tunnel.

"You're not going anywhere!" Mr. Malgren shouted.

"I'm going *back!*" she screamed—really bellowed. She turned around one last time and looked him right in the eye, shotgun and all. "What do you want? Haven't you had enough? You're insane! I'm going back!"

Mr. Malgren had the most horrible look on his face. I ran over to Cherry myself and grabbed one huge arm.

"Wait a minute!" I said. "We're all getting out. Just give us a minute!"

"I'm not giving you a second!" she screamed. Her face was all wet. Spittle was mixed with blood on her lips. Her breath was terrible. She yanked her arm free with one swing. I flew backward.

"Stop!" Mr. Malgren warned, his voice echoing in the cavern.

She didn't stop. She headed toward the mouth of that pipe. Mr. Malgren went right up behind her, with the shotgun in both hands. I thought he might grab her, or run around and get in front of her. Instead, he pointed the gun at the back of her head. I still thought he might just be making a motion.

He pulled the trigger. There was a tremendous explosion. The whole backside of Cherry's head opened up—everything—in every direction. Blood and brains spattered the walls and floor. Chunks of cement fell, from the vibration or stray shot. Dust rose. Rats streamed out everywhere, in swarms.

Mary started screaming.

"Be quiet!" Mr. Malgren shouted. He turned the gun on her. I got up and grabbed her, holding her mouth so tight that I could have broken her neck. Malgren had an insane look—staring at me holding his daughter. He turned around to make sure Hunk was on this side of him. He looked at Cherry's huge, bleeding body on the floor. Her thighs were quivering under the fatigues.

Hunk stepped forward. He shook his head repeatedly, as if trying to clear the numbness. "You shouldn't . . . ," he began. He blinked both eyes and rolled them. He opened his mouth wide, almost as if he were going to yawn. Then he finished, ". . . kill people."

And he walked toward Mr. Malgren.

"Get back!" Mr. Malgren said, and aimed the gun at Hunk.

Hunk just kept shaking his head, like a final, terrible No. "You shouldn't kill people," he repeated in that strange hollow voice. "You shouldn't kill anything."

"Hunk!" I shouted.

"I'm warning you!" Mr. Malgren bellowed. He was shaking with fury. Hunk kept advancing.

There was that same terrible explosion again, with the dust and flying spray. Hunk's big hands went to his stomach. He bent over in horrible pain, but he still kept walking. The blood ran out through his fingers. He raised his hands slightly. Mr. Malgren was reloading the shotgun frantically. He had it in position again when Hunk toppled over on him—hands, arms, legs—his entire body. There was another explosion, and Hunk's big bulk shuddered, but he took Mr. Malgren down with him to the ground. He actually covered Mr. Malgren with his giant body. Blood was in Mr. Malgren's eyes, and the shotgun swung out wildly in his one free arm.

I ran for the arm with the gun. Malgren saw me coming and pointed it at me. Hunk pinned the arm down as well as he could, but he was slipping in his own blood.

"Run!" Hunk said. He was looking straight at me—but the old Hunk eyes were glazed now and bloodshot. "Run!" he repeated.

I did. I grabbed Mary and jumped off the cement ledge onto one of those overturned sections. Then the next—and the next—exactly as the man had earlier. When Mary slipped, I grabbed her and yanked her up and forward. I didn't look back; I didn't look down. We got to the other side of the pool and ran around behind the little round building with the handrails. We still didn't stop. There was a huge pile of stacked pipes. We climbed those and ducked deep behind the highest. Only then did we stop for a second, gasping, and look back.

Mr. Malgren was still down there, but he looked very far away now, maybe because of our height. He seemed dazed. He was trying to get up. Hunk was pushed way over to one side, but Mr. Malgren was still having trouble. He seemed to be wounded. He finally managed to stand weakly, almost on one leg. He peered around unsteadily. He looked right up at us, but he didn't seem to see us. He looked everywhere else, too, with the shotgun hanging in one arm. He didn't seem to know quite what to do, confused and covered with blood.

He gazed around one last time, and then laid the shotgun down on the ground. He limped over to Cherry's body. He bent over and took both her arms and began to pull her slowly, with terrible effort, to the edge of the tank. When he had her right on the ledge, he got around to the other side and pushed. She went over with an enormous splash. Then he went over to Hunk and began the same slow dragging. Before he even had Hunk near the edge, the surface of the water was moving. Then it was alive with splashing. You couldn't really see anything but the foam and movements in the water, but something was hitting the body from every direction.

When Hunk's body went in, the same thing started again—splashing, and the distinct sound of snapping and gnashing. A smell seemed to rise, too—a putrid, decayed stench even worse than the raw sewage smells. Cherry's body was pulled right under. Hunk's took longer, but finally it was dragged under, too.

Holding his gun, Mr. Malgren stared up into the darkness as though he didn't know quite what to do. It was strange to see him that way—limping, covered with blood, and confused. It was the first time I'd ever seen him unsure of himself.

"Mary!" he shouted up into the darkness, as if she might answer.

She started shaking at my side. I pressed her hand. Malgren's voice sounded very close, as if he were just a few feet away.

"Mary!" again.

Again no answer.

"All right," he said. "That's fine. I'll leave you with your friend." But still he waited, as if he believed she might really come out of hiding.

"You're in good company," he added. His voice sounded weak, as if he was almost at the end of his endurance. "All three of you." That put a little chill in me. "You're all alike. Sneaks and liars. Have a good time. . . ." Then he just stood there, an exhausted little man.

Then he tried again—suddenly—hysterically.

"Mary!" He was almost crying. It was probably the first time in his life he'd ever called her and knew she'd heard, without her answering. Mary trembled even harder at my side. You could see the struggle in her, from years of conditioning.

"All right," he said then. "I've got a friend, too."

That's all. And maybe a kind of laugh, or nervous cry. Then he turned around with the gun, stooped down, and crawled back into the pipe.

"Who's his friend?" I asked in a low, very tired voice.

She answered just as wearily. "Queenie, I think."

I almost laughed, despite it all.

"You'd be surprised," Mary said. "You've never seen her when she's tracking something. . . ."

Suddenly I could imagine.

"Let's get out of here, then," I said. We got up and started crawling higher.

Twenty-four

It was a small mountain of pipes, stacked and banded together in groups. We went as high as we could. There was a catwalk just above us, but we didn't use it. We were too exhausted. Instead, we crawled inside a top pipe for a while, to rest.

"Just five minutes or so," I said. I cradled her head in my lap. I might as well have said five seconds, or five hours. Her eyes closed the instant she lay down.

Sitting as quietly as I could, I stroked her hair. It was a large concrete cylinder, and not that uncomfortable. You could hear every sound, no matter how far. That was good. It would give us warning, if he came.

"Mary," I said. Her big eyes opened slightly. "Don't fall asleep. We've got to get out of here before he comes back."

"All right," she answered, but then her eyelids closed again. You could see the blue vein in her temple throbbing. Tears were coursing down her face. She looked drugged—completely wiped out. Her skin was bluish, and one of her breasts was

168

exposed. Her mouth was partly open. She never moved an inch, a dead weight in my lap.

"Do you know who might be down here, to make him that afraid?" I asked. I covered her breast.

"No," she said in a deathly whisper.

"Does he have any enemies?"

"No."

"Has he ever had any trouble?"

"No."

"Office politics? The union maybe?"

"I don't think so."

"Things can get pretty ugly in unions sometimes. . . ."

She seemed to be trying to think, even with sleep pushing in at her. "He's not very active," she said. "He doesn't have any friends, or enemies. No one. Just the dog and the house. Ever since my mother left."

I stroked her hair and let her sleep. It was odd. Even now, after all this, I still couldn't get her to come out with anything against him. Maybe she just didn't know anything. Maybe she never would. She'd always been cooped up in her shell. Beautiful, but a weak beauty. It made me want to protect her, but it never gave me any kind of confidence. She looked pathetic lying on the concrete in that makeshift dress, with her scratched legs, her mouth partly open. . . . Not a girl, and not a woman.

Her head moved. It pushed my jacket aside. The small bundle of papers that I'd picked up in the cellar earlier stuck out. Labels and torn scraps, tied with an old string. I'd forgotten about them. I pulled them out.

The string was so rotten that it broke in my fingers while I was trying to untie the knot.

There was no light, and yet somehow I could see. Maybe because I'd become accustomed to the dark, or maybe from some kind of reflection somewhere. By slanting the paper and looking hard, I could just make out the writing again. But some of the pieces didn't seem to have writing at all—just slashes, like a code or a child's scrawl. Some looked almost Chinese or Eastern—completely indecipherable. The pieces of paper were in various stages of decay, some with the edges eaten away by rats or insects, some stained, and some like ash—flaking apart right in my fingers. Some written with pen, and some with a substitute—a burnt stick, or oil, or dirt. I looked for the one I'd been able to read earlier.

I found it.

before I go crazy

in fairly good handwriting. But then there was a slash and a fierce smudge, as though the writer couldn't control his own fingers. I couldn't help but connect the spastic running and the shrieks and strange noises from white hair and rags.

hiding down here

another one said. Something about *hiding down here*. The rest was lost again, as if he could go maybe three to four words at a stretch. The words on the next didn't follow at all. Something about eating. But finally I arranged three pieces that had more continuous writing than the others. I had to guess sometimes, when the hand lost control, but most of it was readable.

Too readable.

> *Basil Malgren murderer*
> *140 Lincoln Place*
> *KE 1-1733*

Mary's address. Mary's phone number. Basil Malgren, her father.

> *B. brought our bodies down here. I woke up in the water shot in the face and neck but I could breathe. I crawled out and hid.*

Ripped.

I found other ones that might connect. The one about eating, *eating trash* it might have said. Something and something *a long time*.

> *engineer. I couldn't talk. I waved. He came back with B. I hid again. B. shot him just like me and Maurice.*

Another jumble. My eyes ached from trying to make it all out. Most of it was guesswork anyway.

> *hunts for me with the dog*

Another with just the name, over and over:

> *Basil Basil Basil Basil Basil Basil*

Some stray words, decipherable: *head, hurt, breathing,* and *Maurice* again. And *M.* Then that first one,

> *before I go crazy*

Maurice? He killed someone named Maurice.

"Mary," I said. She stirred, as though listening. "Who's Maurice? Do you know a Maurice? Or did you?"

Her eyes opened. She was thinking, or trying to.

"No," she finally answered. "I don't think so."

"Are you sure?"

"Pretty sure."

I let it go. I went through the slips again, trying for additional readable words. . . .

There was a sound.

I listened. A definite sound. A kind of snorting, or rough breathing, like an animal.

I put the papers away. I prodded Mary. She'd heard it, too. Her eyes were wide open. She sat up without saying a word.

Now it was more a moan or whine.

"Queenie?" I whispered.

"I don't think so," she said.

It stopped.

It started again.

It was getting closer. There was the sound of footsteps, and then the snorting and gagging again. Then high-pitched wheezing, and cries. It wasn't human. Not really. Now a long sigh, with a whistling. It seemed very close, but just how close it was hard to say. Everything seemed close down here.

Suddenly there was a terrific shriek—then a squeal, like the sound of a small animal being caught, or killed. Scuffling. Mary was huddling close to me now. I held my hand lightly to her mouth, so she wouldn't speak. It was right outside our pipe, or very near. Someone was walking unevenly and breathing heavily, like a cripple. I pushed Mary into the corner and lay as flat as I could.

I knew who it would be even before he passed the mouth of the pipe, but I still was somehow surprised. White hair and rags, hunched and shaking, carrying a squirming rat on the end of a spear. He glanced in as he passed, but he didn't really see. It was the first time I was able to get a good, hard look at his face. It was the same person who'd killed Krevitch, but somehow it wasn't a horrible face. More like the suffering face of someone who'd been tortured and crippled. The face of the person who'd written—or tried to write— those pathetic notes. He looked weak and confused—and blind, too, or very weak-eyed.

I didn't feel fear at all suddenly. I felt pity. And with it, something else: alliance against Mr. Malgren.

I made sure he was well past the entrance of the pipe. Then I whispered to Mary, "Let's follow him. I want to know what's going on."

She surprised me. Her eyes were huge and blue and expressionless, and she was still trembling, but she answerd, "I do, too."

Twenty-five

You could see him clearly in the dark. It was as if he were coated with phosphorescence, as if he'd accumulated some kind of chemical glow from all his time down here.

We gave him plenty of distance. He wasn't in a hurry. He stopped once to listen to something. Then he jabbed down into a crevice, and there was that squealing again, followed by the hoisting of a small animal high into the air. He pushed it into a sack. Then he swung the sack against the side of a pipe—hard—and the squealing stopped. He slipped the bag over one thin shoulder and hobbled on. All his movements had that same crippled appearance, as if he couldn't quite coordinate. He looked around carefully a few times, but even when he looked back directly, we could tell he was straining and couldn't see that well. We could hear his breathing clearly, even in the distance—short, husky gasps with the strangest whistling and wheezing in between.

I woke up in the water shot in the face and neck

He stopped by an opening. He looked around

carefully. Then he slipped through. It was a wide, open passageway; it wasn't hidden, like the other one. It was probably what he'd retreated to since the invasion of his home.

We waited a while. Then we edged forward.

There was the throb of engines again; perhaps we were near the treatment plant.

I kept Mary way to one side. I moved through the opening. It was another one of those vaults, only noisier. There seemed to be some direct connection to the main pipes here. There were all kinds of huge handwheels every few feet, connecting Y-valves and T-valves. There were gauges and meter boxes. A metal-grating walkway, like a miniature bridge, led past the pipes to an inner room.

He was back there. He had a fire going again, maybe trying to get his dinner together a second time. The noise from the machinery might have made him careless, or maybe he was just too hungry to worry now. You could make out his movements by the shadows on the wall, the same jerky movements as ever. And some kind of weird whining or moaning, too. I listened hard. It was as impossible to decipher as the handwriting. First it seemed like laughter. Then it seemed like singing. Then it was as if a child were playing on a flute or some other musical instrument, hitting various notes at random. There was no pattern and no one sound. Just when you thought you heard giggling, there was that low, husky breathing again—and a wheezing. Then the cough, which turned to whistling.

I walked slowly, carefully, across the grating. His back was toward us. The rags on his body were literally rags—pieces of material tied together in every conceivable way. The remains of a pair of pants were held up by a piece of flapping plastic bag. An old shirt was tied to two or three women's nylon stockings, which were attached to a torn towel on the other side.

I edged forward for a better look at his face. He was defective, you could see that. The eyes were completely vacant, and he drooled long strings of saliva onto the floor. He wore a meaningless smile, and kept making those random snorkling sounds. He was skinning the rat, cutting the hide off the body with a piece of broken bottle. He dropped bits of hide and hair on the floor as he worked. He slit the stomach with the piece of glass, and pulled out the small slippery inside organs with his fingers. He held one of the dark red pieces up for an instant—the liver?—and then in one quick motion tilted his head backward and dropped it in. Some went down his cheek, but most of it ended up in his mouth. He blinked both large vacant eyes, and chewed quickly, and smiled. Then he began that strange series of snorts and grunting again, as though it was hard to get the food down. I couldn't see that closely, but there seemed to be something in his throat—a wound, but not bleeding. Healed, but open. The sounds seemed to be coming from that. He held his neck with one hand when he swallowed.

I moved back to Mary.

"I'm going in there," I whispered. "He's not that big. And he's crippled." I reached down and put a piece of brick in her hand. "Just in case. If I have trouble, help." She looked absurd holding that brick, but she nodded. And she held on to it.

I made my way back to the room. All of his attention was still on the rat. He was now skewering it onto a stick. It was giving him some trouble. It was the perfect moment to slip into the room behind him.

The closer I got, the tinier he looked. And the weaker. It was strange. I couldn't quite identify the feeling—a kind of pity. He was actually skinny and short. I kept thinking of an undernourished teenager—a boy. The hair, which had looked so wild and insane, was actually flaxen and fine in the light of the fire, almost like Mary's hair. The shoulders were narrow. The arms had no muscles at all. I didn't feel remotely afraid suddenly, even after what had happened to Krevitch.

I took a step forward.

His face shot up straight. He sniffed the air. He sensed me. His whole body went rigid. The stick fell from his hands. He spun around.

He shrieked—the most terrible scream. A high whistling came from his throat, and both hands flew up, holding nothing. He jumped backward, hunched and ready.

"Please," I said. I held both hands out, so he

could see that they were empty. "I'm not here to hurt you."

He didn't hear me. Maybe he couldn't. His frightened eyes looked right and left behind me. He began crouching lower and lower, like an animal, until both hands were actually touching the ground. He kept moving backward, toward the wall. I thought he was just retreating. . . .

I advanced, with my hands still open and empty. I even tried to smile. I didn't understand why he was moving backward so steadily until I dropped my eyes. His hands were hovering over a pile of stacked rocks. One hand dropped, and then the other. Both came up with rocks. The right arm went backward in an awkward, wild movement.

"Watch out!" Mary screamed from behind me.

I ducked. The first one went flying over my head and smashed behind me. The second one just missed my shoulder. Both sent me down, which was all the time he needed to reload and keep throwing—two more, and then two more. One finally caught me in the stomach and knocked my wind out. The next one smashed into my leg. I went back against the wall, and down on the floor.

That's all he was waiting for. He ran over and picked up a sharpened construction rod. Then he was right on top of me, that spear in both hands— exactly as he'd been on top of Krevitch.

Twenty-six

Suddenly he screamed.

He froze.

He dropped his spear, and fell backward.

Mary must have thrown the brick. He was gasping and holding his shoulder. I had all the time I needed to grab the spear and get up.

He staggered back to the rock pile. He started throwing again, wildly—hysterically—completely off-target—filling the entire chamber with flying rocks. The barage lasted over a minute, with stones bouncing and ricocheting off every wall.

"We're not here to hurt you!" I shouted again. "We're here to help you!" A chunk of cement just missed my face. He kept throwing and panting—choking and gasping. When he was out of rocks, he started in with whatever was stacked—pieces of pipe, wood, scrap iron, even a nail keg. Then he took a can of oil with a rag wick and threw that. It splashed against the wall and sent flames up the rock, with thick black smoke. But there was nothing for the flames to catch. The oil burned off the rock, and the flames burned out.

In the smoke and confusion, he ran out through the back.

"Come on!" I called to Mary. I chased him. He couldn't run very fast—and he seemed totally disoriented, now. I could see him just ahead, stumbling and tripping.

When I caught him, he was trapped—flush up against a locked steel door. He was out of breath and bent over, holding his neck with one hand as if something was stopping his breathing. When he saw me, he tried to stand upright again. The other hand held a weapon of some kind—a pipe with a piece of broken beer bottle jammed into the opening. But he couldn't breathe. He was choking. One hand went up to his neck again while he stood there, facing off.

"Careful," I warned Mary behind me. I advanced slowly.

He made one last try, lunging at me with the knife. He just missed my arm. I slapped the weapon away. It flew off against the wall, and that seemed to finish him. His breathing turned into steady choking and gagging. He slipped to his knees and toppled over on one side.

"Keep behind me," I told Mary. I didn't trust him. I stood still a second, to be sure. He was lying on the ground, gasping for air. I couldn't help but think of the fish from earlier, grounded and gulping. His color was almost purple. There was a small livid hole in his throat, just under the jaw. It was an old wound, with the edges healed and turned out. I could hear the air sucking through it, and see bubbles of phlegm and blood.

And something else, through the pieces of rags and plastic tied together over the upper portion of the body. . . . At first I thought I was mistaken. I looked again. I wasn't. It was a breast. Two breasts, small and wrinkled and heaving.

It was a woman.

We'd been fighting a woman.

I tried to connect Mr. Malgren with a woman.

Mrs. Malgren.

B. brought our bodies down here.

I went numb. I tried to think—re-think.

It came out the same way again. Mrs. Malgren.

Mary's mother.

Suddenly I even knew exactly who Maurice was.

"It's a woman . . . ," I said to Mary.

"A woman?" She came closer.

I kept waiting for her to see. To recognize her. To say something. She didn't see anything, or recognize anything. Not immediately. Yet the hair was Mary's hair, the same bone-blonde color. And the huge ice-blue eyes were the color of moonstones. . . .

I could breathe. I crawled out and hid.

"Where did she come from?" Mary asked. She really didn't get it. She was in that horrible trance she'd been in half her life. While the old woman just writhed like a hurt animal, with froth coming out of her wound.

B. shot me and Maurice.

Mr. Amour. Maurice. The French teacher. The name I used to laugh over. I could see Mr. Malgren so clearly suddenly, on his hands and knees in that bedroom, with the scrub brush and bucket. . . .

Basil Malgren murderer
140 Lincoln Place

"Mary," I began. She looked at me. She wasn't quite there, maybe from all the terrible years with her father.

"What was Mr. Amour's first name? The French teacher."

"Who?"

"The man your mother ran away with. What was his first name?"

"I don't know."

"Maurice?"

She seemed totally spaced, confused. "I don't . . . Yes. That's right. Maurice. Why?"

She looked at me, and she looked at the woman.

I couldn't say it.

She looked again. She didn't get it.

Then she did.

*

She stared at the woman a long time, numbed the way I'd been numbed. You could see it all registering—the eyes, the hair, the body. But you could also see that something wasn't registering. She looked at the huddled figure, but she wouldn't go any nearer.

"He shot them both," I said in the silence. "Your mother and Mr. Amour. Mr. Amour died, but she lived. . . ."

I waited for some response.

Nothing.

She wasn't listening, or couldn't. She looked so completely alone and so desolate that I suddenly had the feeling she'd lost her mind too—and that nothing I now said would reach her.

I took out the scraps of paper to show her. She ignored them. But something did reach her, finally. She started moving toward the woman.

When the woman saw her coming, she stared up in terror, gasping. Mary reached out slowly, hesitantly, and touched her. The woman flinched as if she'd been burned. She cried out pitifully. Then she glanced off, still gasping, maybe looking for a place to run. She was soaked in perspiration and giving off a strong smell, even down here.

Mary's mouth moved, but no sound came. The tears were starting again. They started in my own eyes, too, and my throat began to ache.

"That's why she's been hiding," I said. "The one time she did wave someone down, it was that engineer. And your father killed him."

The old woman's eyes rolled up at Mary as if she understood what I was saying. But then they rolled off into space again.

Mary reached down to her again, and this time
the old woman didn't flinch so fiercely. Mary's
hand stayed. She stroked the woman's thin shoulder where she'd struck her with the brick, the way
you might stroke a dog you weren't sure of. There
was still some terrible doubt, or distance. The
body and face of her mother must have been
changed incredibly. You could see Mary's mind
going back, too, to the afternoon when she came
home from school to be told that her mother had
run off with the French teacher. . . .

This time she did start to cry. She fell down on
her knees and held the woman to her, like a baby.
She squeezed her until the old woman could
barely breathe, burying the frightened, wrinkled
face in her breast. She cried loudly—confusing the
woman completely. She was trying to say something through the breath and tears, but you
couldn't understand what. She even looked her
mother right in the face and began to speak. But
all that came were more tears, everything breaking down. I kept watching the old woman's face
for some sign of recognition, but just when I
thought there might be something, the vacant
look came back into those blue, bloodshot eyes.
The woman just gasped for more breath, faster,
through that gaping wound in her neck.

Finally Mary said something I could make out.

"You don't recognize me, do you?" She held her
breath for a second, to control the tears. But the
woman kept trembling and breathing hard. She
wouldn't look at her daughter. Her eyes were run-

ning, but everything else was too—her mouth, nose, even that wound. Then Mary started crying again, even harder, holding her mother even closer—so desperately that you could really feel, suddenly, the source of the pain in her. She needed her mother to hold her, too.

But the older woman simply wasn't there anymore.

Mary held her mother for a long time. I kept praying for some kind of change on the old face, some expression or sign. There wasn't anything at all.

Then there was. Something. The breathing changed to high, quick whistles. The eyes changed—rounder and brighter. The old woman seemed to be trying to say something—trying to rise or speak. She was all spastic movements again, and underneath you could hear a low, deep growling—such a confusion of movements and sounds and expressions that I didn't get any of it for a second, and neither did Mary, although both of us knew something was happening. We both thought the noises were coming from the woman. Even when I sensed them behind me, I still thought that they were somehow coming from her, echoing off the stone walls.

Then Mary looked up and beyond me, and I turned, following the direction of her eyes. We all stood and stared.

Queenie, the bulldog, was standing on a small ledge no more that ten feet away—poised and growling, teeth bared, ready to leap.

Twenty-seven

"Don't move," I said. None of us did—not even Queenie. She remained hunched over the ledge, a solid statue of muscle. The black sacks on each side of her mouth were dripping. She looked ten years younger. The deadly growl ran like a small motor deep in her neck.

Then, from outside, came a sound even worse.

"*Queenie!*"

Silence. Just that low, steady growling from the dog.

"Don't move," I said again, "and she won't spring."

"*Queenie—come here!*"

The old lady did move. She started to shake and whimper—actually whining—with the strangest look on her face.

Something changed in the dog then. The hard, bloodshot eyes softened, and the growling died. The ridge on its mangy back went down. It fixed its eyes on the old woman, and the old woman fixed her eyes on the dog. In fact, the old woman's eyes suddenly seemed exactly like the dog's—big and confused, but now gentle. She was dripping

from the mouth, too—just as Queenie was—and
the low rasp coming from the wound in her throat
seemed the same pitch as the dog's.

"*Queenie!*" Mr. Malgren called again—loudly
now, and very near—right outside the passageway.
"Goddammit!"

The woman made a sound. It might have been
the name Queenie, or it might have been a whimper. But she moved, and the dog lunged forward.
I thought the dog was attacking, but instead she
rammed her old wet muzzle right into the old
lady's face, as she stooped, and began to lick
her hands—mouth—throat—the wound—everything.
The old lady began to pet the dog back and
nuzzle her, squeezing her with both old arms—
then licking her! Soon they were both whimpering
and pawing and licking each other, and she was
smiling broadly—actually grinning—with tears
running down her face.

"*Queenie.*" Mr. Malgren was in the corridor between the two rooms. He kicked a can; he seemed
to be stumbling over the scattered rocks. You
could hear him breathing and cursing. Then more
walking. The crunch of his boot heels on the dirt
and sand carried into our room. The old woman's
eyes grew terrified again, and in that one instant,
I think, she finally knew we were all in this together.

"*Fucking cunt!*" Mr. Malgren said, coming into
the entranceway, with no idea that any of us were
in there. "*I'll kill you, too, when I catch you.*"

He walked into the room. We were all huddled

against the far wall. We didn't know what else to do. I don't think he believed his luck. The tiny hairy man stood with his mouth open. He'd changed his clothes, and the gun was a pistol now.

"Well, son of a bitch," he said. He actually smiled—the most hideous smile—staring at the dog crouched in the old woman's arms. He looked at them both, a long time. "So you're all the same," he finally said. "Even the dog. Sneaks and liars."

He raised his gun.

Queenie lunged—just like a three-year-old—warts, wounds and all. The look on Malgren's face was shock—total surprise. He even stammered something, but too late. The dog pounced on him, clamping its yellow teeth into his wrist. Mr. Malgren's bad leg gave and they all went over—Malgren—dog—and the gun, shooting. Complete pandemonium. The richocheting bullets sent up sparks and dust and spray. Mr. Malgren kept cursing, and Queenie kept growling and hanging on. Malgren smashed at the dog with his one free hand and crawled back up on his feet, limping and dragging the dog with him. He backed up toward the entranceway, fighting the animal.

Someone tugged me. It was the old woman, pulling me away. There was a large metal pipe running the whole length of the back wall. Mary was already there. There was a kind of hatch on the side, with a huge handwheel. The old woman took the wheel in both hands and began to struggle with it; she knew it well. It turned and the hatch opened, like something on a submarine.

It was large enough for a body, easily. She climbed up into the pipe, agile as a young girl. She smashed her arm on the side, and the hollow sound of bone on metal rang out, but she never paused.

Mary climbed in next. I followed. There was a noise directly behind us—coming up so close and fast that I didn't even want to look. I yanked the hatch shut. It jammed. Something dark and hairy was caught in it—and there was a terrific, high-pitched shriek. I thought it was Malgren's hand—or head—and I was going to use my fist. Then I realized it was Queenie. I pushed the hatch back open and the old dog lunged up and in. I pulled the hatch shut again, and this time it closed. I held it shut from the inside—tight—using my feet against the side of the pipe for leverage.

There was terrible shouting from outside—just an inch or two away—however thick the walls of that iron pipe were. It was Malgren, pounding on the metal. There was a smashing *clang*, like a clapper hitting the side of a huge bell. It rang right through us—into us. My teeth ached, and my head throbbed. He kept pounding. He was using a pipe or wrench, maybe smashing on that handwheel, trying to open the hatch. Something finally broke. You could hear pieces of metal hitting the floor—and more cursing. Now he seemed to be using his bare hands. There were grunts and squeaks. Then he shot at the wheel. I never budged. I jammed my feet against the side of the pipe—harder—and hung on with both hands.

He stopped.

I held on harder than ever. Mary and her mother and the dog were all perfectly still, waiting.

"How long do you think you can stay in there?" He sounded hysterical—apoplectic.

No answer. Nothing.

"Another five years?"

Silence.

"Is that what you want?"

Just the dog breathing, and the old lady. There was blood all over the inside of the pipe walls—the dog's. She'd been shot.

"All right, bastards. Do you know where you are? The flush pipe! I'll throw the water valve! Is that what you want? Or are you coming out?"

Nothing.

"All right then." There was a pause—then a new sound, a strained, rusty squeaking. He was turning the handwheel on the hatch to lock it.

Then more muttering, and the sound of his boots walking away.

We all waited to be sure.

That old woman began breathing again—terribly, with all that snorting and whistling. Queenie picked up the same rhythm. Even Mary, it seemed.

I pushed on the hatch. It was locked.

The old lady picked it right up. She started to crawl away furiously. The dog followed. Then Mary, then me. The inside of the pipe was slick—

as glazed as pottery. It made it hard to get traction.

No more than half a minute passed before the other sound came—a cranking, as if someone were turning on a huge, ancient radiator.

Then a sizzling, like steam.

"Fast!" I said, smashing into Mary. "Move!"

The smell came, followed suddenly by a horrible icy feel to the pipe. I was the last one in line, so the water touched me first—a cold puddle, washing over my feet and knees and the tops of my hands. Then more of a running stream.

Then hard, in a roar.

Twenty-eight

"Hang on!" I shouted. That just made things worse. The water built up against our bodies and started rising—smashing against us and foaming over our shoulders. Only the dog seemed to be doing all right, paddling and just going with it.

I took the cue. "Let go!" I shouted. I pushed Mary. "Float with it!" She did. She started to move. She must have bumped the old lady free, too. We all started moving with the water, washing on through. The level dropped immediately—to about a half-pipe—and the slick inside surface actually made it easier, then, to move.

I flattened out on my stomach. So did Mary—and even the old lady, for all her spastic flailing. It was as natural as that dog-paddle. We floated through the pipe like debris. We'd crash into the side occasionally, but then we'd push off again. The rush of water helped us keep afloat.

The dog was way ahead now, followed by the old lady, then Mary, then me. It was exactly like the train ride earlier—and the elevator—moving with no control or idea of your own direction. The one difference this time was the noise—the din of water crashing over and under, and the echoes and clanking, and somewhere—outside or inside or underneath—giant turbines or generators growing louder as we moved, so that finally we couldn't have heard each other even if we'd screamed. It was pitch black now, too, so you never knew whose body it was you were bumping, whose cries, whose gasping.

Suddenly changing to—light! I was next to Queenie. I could see her paddling. Queenie, brown and bloody. Natural light—honest to God outside natural light—weak at first, but growing as we floated on. I couldn't remember when we'd last seen light. It was up ahead—at the end of the pipe—some outlet, first about the size of a dime, then a volleyball, and growing. The pipe was emptying into something. The roaring increased, and so did the light. It sounded like a waterfall. It was a waterfall—a drop-off into what looked like a swimming pool the size of a football field, with something like a merry-go-round in its center, turning slowly, spraying water and roaring.

Just as we got to the edge, the old lady panicked and tried to hang on, to keep from washing over. She blocked us all, and the water started to build up again. It smashed us, first to one side, then the other. It crashed over our heads and into our mouths. The old woman didn't look as if she could hang on much longer, but she didn't look as if she'd let herself drop over the edge of that pipe, either. We couldn't stay in there, and we couldn't go back.

The drop into the pool was maybe fifteen feet.

"Let go!" I yelled, so loud that something in my throat ripped. They couldn't hear me. I couldn't hear myself. A wave of water crashed into my open mouth and made me gag. I motioned. I pushed. No one would move, or could move. Everyone was terrified—frozen. There was nothing to do but push Mary aside—and the dog aside—and rip the old lady free from the edge of the pipe. I did. Then I pushed her over. I pushed the dog over. I pushed Mary over. I waited a second, with the water crashing around my shoulders, while they cleared the area below.

Then I went over myself.

I hit thick water and debris. I could smell chlorine. But it was a soft landing, and I was floating. Mary was way over at the base of the thing that looked like a merry-go-round. Her mother was off to another side, clinging to the back of Queenie, who seemed perfectly in control, wounded or not.

The noise was impossible—turbines, all reverberating, with the gigantic machine in the center, spewing water in all directions. The ceiling was miles of skylights. As I stared upward, the spinning machine—the sand filter?—dropped an avalanche of water in my direction. It doused me and sent me under.

I came up choking, with stinging eyes, but I did come up. I swam out of the radius of the machine and tried to find a ladder—a ledge—some way up the side of the mammoth tank. I saw cement steps, finally, leading up and out—and a huge rubber hose above a sign:

EMERGENCY FACE AND BODY BATH

I knew exactly where we were. The treatment plant proper. The main area, the tour area. People. Staff. Freedom.

There! Two city workers—engineers—in uniform—over toward the center, just walking. One of them had a clipboard, and the other was talking and gesturing.

"Hey!" I shouted—jumping up out of the water. I forgot there was nothing under me. I sank back down under. I came up coughing. They couldn't hear me, of course—I could barely hear myself. I shouted again. Mary had seen them too and was over on the far side, waving and shouting. Even the old lady was waving, hanging on to the dog with her other hand. The engineers were so far away that they looked like miniatures. But they just couldn't hear.

One of them finally turned around. A black man. I waved and jumped again, but he couldn't see me. Or if he could, to him I was just something floating in the pool—a board or piece of debris. He turned around again, and they both concentrated on something on the wall—a dial or meter.

I finally reached those steps. I scrambled up as fast as I could. They were slippery with scum, and I fell. I half-crawled up them. I reached the ledge and stood up. I hadn't stood up in so long that my body throbbed and my head started spinning. When I looked back, Mary and her mother and the dog were all down in one section, hanging on to the side, watching me.

I couldn't see the workmen. They were on the other side of that spinning machine. I wasn't even sure now how to get over there. The tank was riddled with walkways and handrails, tunnels and roundabouts and landings. It was hard to tell what led to where.

I followed one route around. It took me almost inside the machine and had me running past huge greasy wheels—dodging axles and blades. The noise was so piercing that I had to cover my ears. But when I did I couldn't keep my balance, so I had to drop my hands again.

Water spray rose like fog, and the stench of chlorine was suffocating. My eyes were burning and I could barely breathe. My side stabbed. I looked down and discovered I was running with no shoes and only one sock. Both feet were bleeding.

They weren't there. When I got around to the other side where that meter was, they weren't there! I looked back at where I thought Mary and her mother were. They were way back—farther— like tiny dolls, by the ledge of the pool. They were waving, motioning with their arms, but I couldn't tell why. I looked up and down.

I saw the two engineers again. They were walking away toward a large, double metal door.

"Hey!" I screamed—really screamed. It was the

same thing again. They couldn't hear me. Maybe they were wearing ear plugs because of the engines. I ran toward the door. There was another maze of handrails and bridges and catwalks. It must have taken me twice as long as it took them to cover the same distance. I kept running into gratings—boilers—chimneys—strange sections and turns.

When I reached the door, it was shut. I smashed at it. I shouted. I couldn't hear my own noise. The big double doors were like a bank vault's—covered with sheet metal and riveted—probably insulated, because of the terrible din. I looked for a buzzer. I looked for an intercom or one of those wall phones—some kind of communication system. All I could see were wires and plugs and meters and cables, switchboxes and button boards.

That was all right. We could come back and pull them—pull them all—the cables and wires and plugs! Pull everything until someone somewhere caught on and came out! At least we were finally above ground! Free! Through the skylights you could actually see white light—the light of early evening, daylight saving time. All the hours in that place, coming to an end. I felt excited—completely energized again.

Mary and her mother and the dog were all out of the pool now and resting on the ledge. I could see them way in the distance. I wanted to shout, but it wouldn't have done any good. All I had to do now was get back to them—and get them back here.

I ran toward them as fast as I could. I could never remember running so fast and sure, or feeling so good. I took those catwalks and detours and ledges and paths as though they were neighborhood sidewalks.

When I got near them, I saw that Mary and her mother looked sick and exhausted. I tried to shout something, but I couldn't. I didn't have any breath left, and the noise was too much anyway. Queenie was on her side, and there was blood all over her body. She looked dead. She was dead. But she'd been wounded—I'd known that. The other two kept staring at the dog, though—even after I'd approached—wearing the exact same defeated expressions.

"We're all right—" I began.

Then I stopped cold.

Queenie had been shot in the head. It was a new wound. There was a hole where her eye had been. . . .

Mr. Malgren moved out from behind a boiler, holding the pistol. "Let's go," he said, or you could see him say, even though you couldn't hear anything over the machines. He motioned toward a little doorway by an elevator. He stood aside so we could all walk ahead.

Mary stood up, shaking. She put her arm around her mother and walked toward the door. I started to follow her, but Mr. Malgren mouthed something else at me.

I didn't get it.

He said it again, pointing to the body of the

dog. This time I got it. I went over and took hold of Queenie's hind legs and dragged her—with great effort—toward the elevator. While I was doing that, Mr. Malgren took the emergency face and body hose and sprayed the blood away.

Then we all got inside, with Queenie at our feet. It was the same elevator we'd used earlier, with the same jimmied slot. Only this time there were keys in the slot, and there was light and power.

Mr. Malgren shut the gate. Then he reached over and turned the key. The door closed, automatically.

Twenty-nine

He took the elevator down without saying a word. His eyes never left his wife's, but she didn't look back. She didn't look anywhere. She just stood there shivering and dripping and covered with debris. Her breathing was worse than ever. It seemed a miracle she was even alive. Mr. Malgren seemed to think so too.

When we reached the bottom, he didn't open the gate. He held the pistol in one hand, and let the other hand rest on the bars.

"I hope you all enjoyed each other's company," he said. When his wife didn't look up or answer, he looked at his daughter. Then at me. He had that same outraged face.

He looked at his wife again. "See what lies do?"

"She can't speak," Mary said.

"Shut up!" He slapped her so hard that she flew back against the elevator and slid down to the floor next to Queenie. "You're a liar too! I've seen it for years! All yes and smiles, but you're a sneak!"

He turned to me with the most hateful eyes. "And you're the reason. There's always someone like you—sneaking into a man's house to ruin it. Intellectuals! Do you know what I did with her French intellectual? Do you know what I'm going to do with you?"

He was actually frothing at the mouth, and his eyes were glazed insanely. He stood there gasping for breath, gesturing, shrieking, like an old film clip of Hitler.

"Ask her!" he screamed at his daughter. "Ask your mother what her French *intellectual* was teaching her! Ask her!" But Mary wouldn't ask her mother anything, or even look up, which made the old man even more furious. When I looked at him and his eyes met mine, there was an instant of total frustration—as if he wanted to shout something more, but couldn't think of what. Then he brought up the pistol and smashed it into the side of my head.

Maybe I was already too hurt. There wasn't as much pain as numbness. I couldn't stand; I couldn't see. I too slipped down to the floor, on top of the dead dog.

"Now you're not so tall—you see?" He kicked me on the other side of the head with his boot. I didn't feel that so much either, but I couldn't see at all now. The gate of the elevator opened. I must have been leaning on it. I fell out, against the door—and when the door opened, out onto the ramp. I could still hear, and I could move a little. I just couldn't see.

"Get up!" he shrieked. He kicked me again. Twice. I could feel the kicks more than the pain.

It was very warm down here—muggy and thick, like earlier, with that same putrid smell. We were back in the Catacombs, the sewer under the sewer.

I did get up somehow.

"Pull the dog," he said.

I had all I could do to find the dog. I couldn't see, but I pulled. At first I could hardly balance myself. Then the dead weight of the dog actually seemed to help me keep my footing. Mr. Malgren's voice seemed close, then far away. We all walked past that old corroded door from earlier. But then we took another route—longer—which ended up at the same pool where we'd left Krevitch and Cherry and Hunk.

"Throw her in," he ordered.

I pulled Queenie as close to the edge as I could without losing my own footing. Her paws kept slipping out of my hands because of the blood, but I finally got her into position. I had blood trickling down my face, and I kept gagging as if I had to throw up, with nothing coming up.

I pushed her in. She went over the edge and hit the water with a loud flop. I watched. Mr. Malgren did too. The body just floated. Nothing came. Maybe they were full.

I was about to look away when I did see something, but not in the water. It was on the ledge beneath me. It was out of Mr. Malgren's line of sight, but I could see it—so large and close that I began to wonder about my eyes. But my eyes were all right now. It was an alligator, more black than brown, and huge, with clear-cut ridges on its back, raised in blocks. It was lying still as could be, with wide-open yellow eyes. Its stomach looked distended on both sides, as if it had eaten heavily. Maybe that's why it was lying there. Somehow it didn't look evil or threatening at all. It looked almost wise. I couldn't look away. Some blood from my head dripped right down on it, spattering into its eyes. Big clear lids, like plastic lenses, rose upward as it blinked the blood away. It opened its jaws slightly, then opened them wider and left them open, showing long rows of bent ivory teeth. But it didn't move.

"You like that?" Mr. Malgren asked me, noticing the direction of my stare. I thought he meant the alligator, but he was just gazing over the steaming, putrid pool. He actually took a deep breath.

"I like it," he said. "I've grown to like this place. It's home now. At least I know what's going on here." He was half talking to himself, as if groggy on sewer gas. "I used to hate the smell of this place. Everyone told me it would get to be second-nature. But you know what? It's first-nature now."

He took another deep breath, as if inhaling the morning air. I looked back down at the alligator. It was staring back up at me, and the jaws were still wide open, like a bear trap.

"It reminds me of the world," he said. "That's why I like it." He looked at his wife, hideous and choking, crouching on the ground. "You used to always love the world, didn't you?" he asked her.

"You were very big on the world." Then he looked at Mary. "Both of you. Well, the world's fine, but people stink!"

He turned back to his wife and shot her. It was so loud, and the vibration came through the concrete so strongly, that I thought he'd shot me. I could feel it.

"This time," he said, as she lay still with the blood running, "stay dead! Stay in there, with your boyfriend! Just stay there!" And he shot her again. She didn't even quiver. She just lay like a rag doll. It almost seemed a relief.

"Pick her up," Mr. Malgren ordered.

I staggered over there. I was dizzy again. I couldn't breathe. I got halfway to the body and collapsed. He kicked me right up again. "Get up, bastard!"

I got up. But it was too much. I couldn't stand. I fell over again, and this time no matter how much he kicked, I couldn't rise. I couldn't even move.

"All right, then. I'll do it myself. But watch me. I want you to see what lies do. She and him are getting together again."

He began to pull the body over to the edge himself, limping. He got it as close as he could. Then he pushed.

It went over the edge, but it didn't go down. One of her tied rags snagged an old jutting brick. She dangled there, light and tiny, like some kind of jinxed doll made to torment him. And it did torment him. He got very excited. He pulled and pushed at the rag with his free hand, but it wouldn't come off the brick.

He put the gun down on the ledge. He used both hands. This time the rag came off and the body shot down. But it still didn't go into the water. It fell on the ledge below.

He was furious. He was standing just over from where I'd seen the alligator, but he didn't seem to notice. He was completely out of control now—gasping and sputtering.

He stepped down onto the ledge on that one good leg, to give the body a last shove. There was a terrific grunt—then a hiss and roar, and the sound of a set of jaws snapping shut—hard.

He screamed.

All you could see were his head and shoulders—and his one arm, reaching hysterically over the ledge for the pistol. But he couldn't quite reach it. He struggled again, and stretched again. His hand was only about two inches away. Then his hand began to drag backward, along with his whole body. The alligator was pulling him in. His fingers clawed at the cement.

"Give me the gun!" he shouted at Mary. "Hand me the gun!"

She looked around for it, confused.

I got up, or tried to get up. The blood rushed to my head. I fell right back down again. I wanted that gun in my hands, not his. I tried to crawl, but I couldn't even crawl. All could was think about crawling, while the blood ran down my face.

"Hand it to me!" he screamed. "On the ledge!

Right there. It's pulling me in! Hand me the gun!"

Mary finally saw it, and staggered over to the pistol. She looked stunned. She reached down, but missed the gun, fumbling first too far left, then too far right.

"Don't," I said—but I could only whisper. I didn't even know if she heard me. "Don't!"

She picked it up. She held it by the barrel, very uncertainly, as if she'd never touched a gun before. She walked with it toward the ledge. Mr. Malgren was in the water now—it was coffee-colored from his blood. The reptile was slowly pulling him farther and farther from the ledge. He stretched out his hand. Mary was right on the edge, close enough to touch him.

"Don't!" I shouted loudly.

She looked at me.

"Don't!" I said again.

She looked as if she couldn't quite focus—understand—hear.

"Mary!" Mr. Malgren shouted. And this time he really did scream—a terrified, final cry as the alligator pulled him down another foot. *"Give me that gun!"*

"It registered. You could see it on her face.

"Don't," I said. *"Mary."*

She looked at him. She looked at me.

"Don't," I repeated.

"Mary!" he screamed.

Something changed in her face. The child went away.

She pointed the gun toward the water.

She fired.

She hit her father. She fired again, and she hit him again. She fired a third time, and she hit him a third time. He was looking right at her as each bullet hit, as if he couldn't quite believe it. Even as the thing pulled him down slowly and steadily, that expression on his face never changed. Even when just his head and shoulders were above water—then his head, then just his eyes—he was still staring at us both with that same incredulous look.

Thirty

"Get up," Mary said. She had one arm under me. Her voice seemed changed—huskier and more controlled.

"Let me lie here a minute."

"We càn't There's a fire."

I looked up. I had to focus my eyes. There were flames shooting up over the pool. But strange flames—isolated—like the flames from gas jets. They licked up off the surface of the water, then they disappeared. Then one would catch farther over, burning blue or yellow or orange for an instant—then disappearing again. It was like the northern lights or some kind of psychedelic show—flames popping up out of the air, out of rock, out of pipes, out of water.

There was a tremendous *whoosh* suddenly. The coupling of a large black pipe sent up a perfect ring of sapphire blue flames, like a huge stove burner.

"It's the methane," she said. "The gunshots set it off. Come on."

She was still remarkably calm. She helped me up. I couldn't see and I couldn't walk, but I saw and I walked as we headed back toward the corridor. There was a sudden blue explosion right in front of our faces—and another orange one farther off, on the wall. You could feel the heat and smell the gas, but it always disappeared as soon as you looked, as if the source were suddenly cut. All except the fire on the joints of that one big pipe, which now shot up broad blue flames.

We started to run.

When we opened the door, the draft must have changed. There was suddenly a whole series of *whooshes* and pops and small explosions behind us, and the air was streaked with flames burning vertically—even laterally—on air currents. We slammed the door shut behind us.

"Hurry!" she said, pulling with real strength.

We got to the elevator. The air was thick with smoke and with a sweetish smell almost like incense. The power was still on in the elevator, exactly as Mr. Malgren had left it. I was praying I knew the buttons. I pulled the gate shut, and then the doors. I swung the wall lever up.

Nothing. Just smoke, filling that cubicle.

I pushed a button.

Nothing.

I held the lever up while I pushed the button, and this time the elevator caught and began to rise. Smoke was rising, too, from the shaft. A flame leaped up at us from under the door exactly as they'd leaped below—with that strange flickering pop before they died out.

"If it catches a pocket of gas," Mary said, studying the wall markings through the glass as we rose, "it'll go." She still was very controlled. She watched those markings as though she knew the entire layout.

There was another explosion—larger than anything earlier. We could feel the elevator rock.

"That's it," she said.

Another explosion. The lights flickered, but the elevator kept rising.

Another—the largest yet, from deep below and right under us. The smoke was different now—oily and more stifling, like burnt rubber.

The lights went out. The elevator stopped.

I waited for that horrible descent again, as when the power had failed earlier. Mary didn't. She began to pry the gate open. Then the door.

"We're not that far from the floor," she said. "Look."

We were, but weren't. There was the main floor, and daylight, just above us—but the elevator had stopped midway. There was a narrow open space visible—and skylights.

"Let's go," she said. She never looked back. She went right to the edge of the elevator floor, overlooking the shaft. She reached out and grasped the oily cable. She pulled her hand back. She yanked off the tablecloth she'd been wearing, wrapped that around the cable and gripped it again, standing there in her panties.

"Can you follow me?" she asked.

"I think so." The smoke was so thick I could barely see her.

She grabbed the cable and leaped. Her foot missed. She slipped. I grabbed her one free-swinging foot and pushed. She had both hands on that greasy cable, gripping and pulling. She stretched up her other leg as high as it would go. I pushed again, and she swung a little. Her foot caught the ledge of the main floor. I pushed again, and this time she had enough leverage to make the span.

She jumped and landed safely.

"Come on," she shouted, throwing me the tablecloth.

I gripped the cable the same way. I took the same leap and swing, but with no one to push me off. When I swung in, she grabbed my free hand. She pulled. I let go of the cable. There was one sickening moment when we both teetered because of the difference in our weights. I actually felt myself falling backward into the shaft. But in that instant the big explosion came—so strong that the force of the blast blew me right over the ledge of the main floor to safety.

Then the elevator went—in a crash—straight down the shaft, never stopping until it hit the ground floor. The sides of the shaft caved in after it. Part of the floor began to cave in, too—where we were huddling. Even the walls.

We ran again. You could feel the entire floor moving as if there were an earthquake. We were in the skylight area again. Glass started to fall, raining down on one side of the plant. There was the sand filter, spinning its water. A second later, it began to rock wildly, and right after that it slowly toppled—in gigantic pieces—down into the pool. The water overflowed, and there were flames and pieces of overturned machinery everywhere.

A boiler exploded. You could see a geyser of steam shooting up through the smoke.

"Over here!" someone yelled. A human voice. It was the black engineer from earlier, standing in the entrance between those big metal double doors. "Hurry!"

We both ran for the big doors. There were two workers—three—with phones ringing and lights flashing, behind them. An alarm was sounding. People never looked so good. We ran through the doors, and the engineers closed them behind us. For an instant they could only stare at us, as if we were from another planet. That's how we must have looked, too—all blood and rags, bruised and choking. We were both blinking from the light.

Fire sirens started—rounds and rounds—and soon the place was filled with raincoats and axes and hoses, police, all kinds of squads of people in a hurry, shouting this, asking that. We both collapsed in a corner and let the bodies mill around us. So many people occupied with so many functions that I almost forgot they'd eventually get around to us. I closed my eyes and tried to rest.

Someone woke me—a doctor giving first aid. There was someone behind us, too—a police officer asking something. He had to ask it twice.

"What were you doing down there?" he repeated.

I swallowed. I looked over at Mary. There was a nurse, or some kind of ambulance attendant, with her, bandaging her hands. She had tears in her eyes, but she still managed to look at me. She looked older but somehow better, even in that condition. She half-smiled. She even gave me a little wink.

I took a deep breath before I spoke. Then I began, very slowly.

"We were on a tour. . . ."

San Francisco
Summer, 1977

ABOUT THE AUTHOR

David J. Michael has his own public relations consulting firm in San Francisco. His first novel. *A Blow to the Head,* received critical acclaim.

Big Bestsellers from SIGNET

☐ **THIS HOUSE IS BURNING by Mona Williams.**
(#E8695—$2.25)*

☐ **THE MESSENGER by Mona Williams.** (#J8012—$1.95)

☐ **PHONE CALL by Jon Messmann.** (#J8656—$1.95)*

☐ **THE LONG WALK by Richard Bachman.** (#E8754—$1.95)*

☐ **RAGE by Richard Bachman.** (#W7645—$1.50)

☐ **SAVAGE RANSOM by David Lippincott.** (#E8749—$2.25)*

☐ **THE BLOOD OF OCTOBER by David Lippincott.**
(#J7785—$1.95)

☐ **TREMOR VIOLET by David Lippincott.** (#E6947—$1.75)

☐ **VOICE OF ARMAGEDDON by David Lippincott.**
(#E6949—$1.75)

☐ **THE EYE OF THE GODS by Richard Owen.**
(#J8849—$1.95)*

☐ **MANHOOD CEREMONY by Ross Berliner.** (#E8509—$2.25)*

☐ **BALLET! by Tom Murphy.** (#E8112—$2.25)

☐ **LILY CIGAR by Tom Murphy.** (#E8810—$2.75)*

☐ **CITY OF WHISPERING STONE by George Chesbro.**
(#J8812—$1.95)*

☐ **SHADOW OF A BROKEN MAN by George Chesbro.**
(#J8114—$1.95)*

* Price slightly higher in Canada

To order these titles, please
use coupon on the next page.

More Bestsellers from SIGNET

- ☐ **EYE OF THE NEEDLE** by Ken Follett. (#E8746—$2.95)*
- ☐ **FLICKERS** by Phillip Rock. (#E8839—$2.25)*
- ☐ **LOVE, LAUGHTER, AND TEARS** by Adela Rogers St. Johns. (#E8752—$2.50)*
- ☐ **MAKING IT** by Bryn Chandler. (#E8756—$2.25)*
- ☐ **DAYLIGHT MOON** by Thomas Carney. (#E8755—$1.95)*
- ☐ **THE RICH ARE WITH YOU ALWAYS** by Malcolm Macdonald. (#E7682—$2.25)
- ☐ **THE WORLD FROM ROUGH STONES** by Malcolm Macdonald. (#E8601—$2.50)
- ☐ **SONS OF FORTUNE** by Malcolm Macdonald. (#E8595—$2.75)*
- ☐ **JO STERN** by David Slavitt. (#J8753—$1.95)*
- ☐ **PHOENIX** by Amos Aricha and Eli Landau. (#E8692—$2.50)*
- ☐ **WINGS** by Robert J. Sterling. (#E8811—$2.75)*
- ☐ **TWINS** by Bari Wood and Jack Geasland. (#E8015—$2.50)
- ☐ **THE KILLING GIFT** by Bari Wood. (#J7350—$1.95)
- ☐ **.44** by Jimmy Breslin and Dick Schaap. (#E8459—$2.50)*
- ☐ **THE INFERNAL DEVICE** by Michael Kurland. (#J8492—$1.95)*
- ☐ **DYING LIGHT** by Evan Chandler. (#J8465—$1.95)*

　　　* Price slightly higher in Canada

THE NEW AMERICAN LIBRARY, INC.
P.O. Box 999, Bergenfield, New Jersey 07621

Please send me the SIGNET BOOKS I have checked above. I am enclosing
$_____ (please add 50¢ to this order to cover postage and handling).
Send check or money order—no cash or C.O.D.'s. Prices and numbers are
subject to change without notice.

Name _____

Address _____

City_____ State_____ Zip Code_____
　　　　　　Allow at least 4 weeks for delivery
　　This offer is subject to withdrawal without notice.